I0630086

Writer Guild of America East
Certified Registration Number: I370871
Date Registered: 05/25/2024
KDP ISBN: 9798326819437

Cover artwork created by ChatGPT 4.0 DALL-E
Printed in the United States of America

... to all those who fight daily to care for the little ones ...

Lethal Mercy

Tito Lugo MD©

I

The dark burden of the soul, that overwhelming weight, resides in the deepest recesses of our minds. So meditated Nurse Amarilis Cintron, whose steps echoed somberly through the illuminated corridors of the neonatal intensive care unit of the brand-new National Pediatric Hospital. Every breath of the newborns, every blink of the monitors reminded her of the fragility of the life that lay in her hands, a constant reminder of her solitary burden and the painful decision she believed it was her moral duty to uphold. Her demeanor, though serene, concealed the storms of a soul divided between duty and mercy, a heart tormented by the struggle between life and the relief of suffering.

The National Pediatric Hospital was situated in a vibrant South American country. It consisted of a majestic structure recently erected to care for a population of half a million souls where one in five breathed the freshness of youth before crossing the threshold into maturity at twenty-one. With an astronomical expenditure of 135 billion pesos, this sanctuary of medicine stood as a bulwark of care from the cradle of the newborn to the gate of the young adult. Armed to the teeth with the most advanced technology, the hospital boasted six operating rooms dedicated exclusively to neonates, all under the watchful eye of the renowned pediatric surgeon, Dr. Heriberto Lucio Vicens, whose fame and expertise echoed through the corridors of this temple of healing.

Dr. Lucio Vicens had dedicated his life to medicine, specializing in general, pediatric, and cardiothoracic surgery. After more than nine years of intense training following his doctorate, he now held an impressive list of certifications. With this background, he came to the island of retirement, a place where resources were limited, and hope was scarce.

Lucio not only brought with him his vast experience but also an almost supernatural mastery of robotic surgery, a skill he had perfected by operating on newborns barely weighing one kilogram. The mechanical arms of these sophisticated devices became his own hands, capable of making minimal incisions of three millimeters to dissect, cauterize, excise, and suture with an almost inhuman precision. From a cabin reminiscent of an airplane pilot's, Lucio controlled every movement, his eyes hidden behind glasses that provided a three-dimensional view of the surgical field.

Despite the high cost the government had invested in this technology, Lucio knew these robots represented the only hope for the tiny patients in the neonatal intensive care unit. However, the metallic gleam of the robotic arms and the cold of the cabin contrasted with the dark reality of the island: a despair that permeated every corner of the hospital. The tiny bodies of the neonates, so fragile and vulnerable, seemed destined for an unequal struggle against fate.

Lucio, aware of the responsibility on his shoulders, could not help but feel like an angel of death, supplanting nature with each cut and suture. Each operation was a macabre dance, a desperate attempt to snatch these babies from the embrace of death, though he sometimes wondered if he was simply prolonging their suffering.

Night fell over the island, and the hospital, shrouded in shadows, seemed like a gigantic specter. The monitors emitted constant beeps, accompanying the irregular heartbeat of the tiny hearts. Amid this somber scene, Lucio prepared for a new intervention, knowing that every time he set the robot in motion, the thin line between life and death became even blurrier.

"Good morning, Nurse Cintron," mumbled Dr. Lucio Vicens as he entered the neonatal intensive care unit (NICU) at seven in the morning. The faint light of dawn was just beginning to filter through the windows, casting elongated shadows on the hospital walls. Nurse Amarilis Cintron, with her slender figure and impeccably arranged hair, had clocked in for work just five minutes earlier.

"Good morning, doctor," she replied with a mischievous look, a spark in her eyes suggesting an interest that went beyond the professional.

"How is the baby I operated on yesterday for tracheoesophageal fistula?" asked Lucio as his eyes scanned the monitors and his nimble fingers reviewed the digital record on the laptop in front of the tiny patient.

"Well, the night shift informed me that after regaining mobility, his parameters are adequate for extubation," replied Amarilis, her voice filling the air with a mix of professionalism and subtle flirtation.

"Perfect! Thank you," exclaimed Lucio with an air of majesty, aware that thanks to his intervention, the baby would soon be able to use his esophagus properly, something fate had denied him at birth.

"Let's move on to the next one," he added, moving towards the next incubator where a 22-week-old, 600-gram baby lay, intubated, and a victim of grade IV intraventricular hemorrhage. This tiny being, more akin to a vegetable than a living entity, was under surgical observation for stage II necrotizing enterocolitis, with a risk of intestinal perforation.

"This baby isn't doing too well," mentioned Nurse Cintron to the prominent surgeon, her tone now laden with concern. "The ventilation parameters had to be increased. He's very sick, doctor," she continued, her voice a whisper that seemed to resonate in the dark corners of the NICU.

"I've reviewed the X-rays on the PC and it still doesn't show signs of intestinal perforation," responded Lucio, his words imbued with a forced calm. "But we will remain vigilant," he added, with a tone that tried to instill hope amidst the despair.

"It will be done, doctor," Amarilis nodded, their gazes crossing once more. This time, the connection was deeper, a silent encounter between their souls that touched the edges of desire, just before the doctor left the NICU.

The atmosphere in the neonatal intensive care unit was heavy, almost tangible, with a mix of hope and despair that clung to every corner. The beeping of monitors and the soft murmur of medical staff created a somber symphony, as life and death danced in delicate balance over the tiny bodies of the neonates.

Amarilis had worked for five years as a pediatric nurse in neonatology. She cared for premature babies from 22 weeks of gestation. The hospital received newborns from all over the country. These babies had a variety of medical and surgical conditions. It was the only supratertiary center in the country, boasting a wide range of medical and surgical specialties.

Amarilis never had a proper childhood. What happened in those early years was a succession of low blows, one after another, without respite. In the house where she grew up, screams were more frequent than conversations, and looks were more of rancor than affection. All of this simmered slowly, in an environment where each day was harder to breathe than the last.

There was no escape or consolation, only the constant hammering of despair and hidden violence. She learned to walk with her head down, to avoid conflicts, and to anticipate the next blow, whether physical or emotional. Her understanding of the world became tinged with this sordidness until pity became her twisted form of affection.

For Amarilis, her actions were not crimes, but a preventive form of care. In her mind, marked by abandonment and brutality, taking life was an act of mercy. She believed that by freeing these beings from their future pain, she was doing them a favor—saving them from a world that had nothing good to offer. She didn't see the light at the end of the tunnel because, in her life, there simply never had been one.

Amarilis had been a victim of her stepfather; her mother, abandoning Amarilis's biological father when she was barely nursing, had plunged from the jaws of one tyrant into the arms of another, worse one. Her natural father was a man prone to violence, a chauvinist who, repressed and corroded by past torments, perpetuated a cycle of suffering. He was a living illustration of a deep-seated cultural pathology that painted men as innate predators of women, an absurd and cruel notion that not even wild animals seemed to emulate.

Faced with such a history, Amarilis sheltered in her own mental labyrinth, avoiding anything that could evoke the memory of those abuses. Enclosed spaces, the exclusive company of male figures, any scenario that exuded the scent of that lived horror, everything was meticulously avoided. Her nights were a theater of nightmares and déjà vu that terrified her, clearly announcing the presence of post-traumatic stress disorder. She felt and suffered a deep fear, an anxiety that consumed her relentlessly. For any observer with a minimum of discernment, the diagnosis was unequivocal.

In each encounter with the gaze of a man who reminded her of her stepfather, Amarilis felt how the past was not a country from which one could flee; it was a specter that pursued her without rest, slipping into every crack of her daily life. She was aware of this fracture within herself, and although she fought to overcome it, the weight of memory and the legacy of her family heritage were heavy burdens to bear. Her life had become a constant balancing act between the desire to forget and the need to remember enough to prevent history from repeating itself.

That was not the case with the surgeon. Amarilis felt a deep admiration and even a passion in her loins for the knowledge and devotion of Dr. Lucio Vicens, who visited the sick babies daily with an almost obsessive dedication. For the young nurse, meeting such an impressive academic magnate amid her life filled with disastrous experiences was a balm. Especially when it came to those babies weighing less than a kilogram, whose fragile and weak bodies seemed to defy the logic of life.

The hospital was filled with palpable pain when the parents, distraught and defeated, some first-timers, approached the incubators. Tears fell down their cheeks as they saw their premature offspring struggling for every breath. Amarilis suffered with them, sharing their pain, a pain that rekindled memories of her own personal hell. Every time a parent cried, it was as if an old wound was reopened, a wound inflicted by her foolish stepfather in her youth.

Amarilis remembered with vivid clarity the nights of terror, the elongated shadows looming over her bed, and her stepfather's sour breath, mixed with the stench of alcohol. Her childhood had been a battlefield, and each visit from her stepfather an assault on her innocence. Working in the NICU offered her a kind of redemption, a desperate attempt to save lives that had not yet had the chance to be tainted by the world's cruelty.

Dr. Vicens's devotion was a beacon in the midst of that darkness. His surgical precision and meticulous calm contrasted with the emotional chaos that reigned in the hospital. Amarilis watched him, fascinated by his ability to operate with an almost inhuman coldness, as if he were a machine destined to defy death. And yet, behind that façade of perfection, she felt there was something more, a spark of humanity he tried to hide under his surgeon's gown.

As parents collapsed in front of the incubators, Amarilis couldn't help but feel a mixture of compassion and despair. Each tear was a reminder that suffering was a constant, a shadow lurking in every corner of the hospital. But it was also fuel, a reason to keep going, to try to pull those tiny beings from the abyss that threatened them.

The light in the NICU was always cold and clinical, accentuating the lines of worry on the faces of those who worked there. The monitors continued their constant symphony, beeps and alarms indicating the critical state of the patients. And in the midst of it all, Amarilis found a kind of solace in the presence of Dr. Lucio Vicens, a man who, despite everything, seemed to have the strength to face the darkness and, if only a little, return hope.

At three in the afternoon, the monitors of the patient with necrotizing enterocolitis fell silent, announcing a sudden cardiac arrest. The ventilation parameters had not shown any changes indicating imminent deterioration, but something had gone terribly wrong. Although the baby was high-risk due to extreme prematurity, no one expected such a sudden turn. In those days, a spontaneous abortion usually referred to a fetus weighing around 500 grams, and this little fighter exceeded that by just 100 grams.

The tiny body of the baby was tinged with a deadly gray color, the clearest sign that he had gone into cardiac arrest and his heart rate had dropped to less than 60 beats per minute. The situation demanded immediate cardiopulmonary resuscitation with medications. Amarilis, though her shift had ended, couldn't leave the NICU at that critical moment. Her sense of duty and her connection to the tiny patients kept her firmly in place.

Amarilis joined the resuscitation team, her movements quick and precise, while her heartbeat with a mix of hope and despair. The unit was immersed in a tense silence, broken only by the short and clear orders of the medical team and the noise of the resuscitation equipment. Every passing second increased the pressure, and after forty exhausting minutes, the decision was made to declare the patient deceased. It was 4:20 PM.

The news fell like a stone on the NICU staff. Dr. Lucio Vicens had to be notified. Amarilis felt as if an invisible hand was squeezing her heart. Although she had witnessed and participated in numerous resuscitations, the loss of a baby was always devastating.

Dr. Lucio Vicens was still at the institution, finishing a delicate case of Fallot's tetralogy through thoracoscopic surgery using his famous robot. The precision of the mechanical arms was almost surgical, moving with an unnatural grace as Lucio controlled them from the cabin, his eyes fixed on the three-dimensional screen that offered him a detailed view of the patient's tiny heart.

Suddenly, the intercom in the room emitted a static crackle before Amarilis's voice filtered through, laden with palpable sadness.

"Dr. Vicens," began Amarilis, her voice barely a somber whisper.

"The baby with necrotizing enterocolitis... had a cardiac arrest. We did everything we could, but..."

The words hung in the air, wrapped in a silence that resonated louder than any scream. As soon as Lucio received the message from the unit, a chill ran down his spine. Without wasting a second, he headed up to the NICU to see what had happened.

Upon arrival, the atmosphere in the NICU was more oppressive than usual, the fluorescent lights flickering as if aware of the horror that had just occurred. The baby's vital signs had shown no warning of deterioration. Lucio reviewed the X-rays with obsessive meticulousness: there were no signs of perforation. The baby had received an intravenous ductus arteriosus blocker five minutes before the arrest, a medication that should not affect the heart rate.

The ventilator parameters had not changed in the last four hours before death, a detail that made the situation even more enigmatic. Everything indicated that something strange and inexplicable had happened. The feeling that a sinister presence was lurking in the corners of the NICU grew stronger.

Lucio was invaded by a growing unease, a shadow of doubt that followed him as he observed the baby's inert body. The grayish skin of the tiny patient seemed to absorb the light, projecting an aura of death that extended throughout the room. Toxicological tests had to be performed to determine if any medication had affected the baby, but the unease persisted. The air was thick with unbearable tension, as if the hospital itself was breathing with difficulty.

Dr. Lucio Vicens was filled with questions, more than he found answers. The unusual death of the baby had no logical explanation. As his thoughts oscillated between science and terror, he couldn't shake the feeling that something dark and malevolent was hiding in the shadows of the NICU, waiting for its moment to strike again. The walls of the hospital seemed to close in, the silence became oppressive, and Lucio felt as if an invisible, malicious gaze was following him with every step he took.

The certainty that he had to face the unknown became clearer. It wasn't just about medicine; something deeper and more sinister was at play. As the murmurs of the monitors and the flickering lights continued their unsettling symphony, Lucio knew this was just the first of many dark nights they would face in the NICU.

It was also necessary to perform an autopsy on the baby. He had died without a sufficient medical explanation, leaving an unsettling unease in the air. The news was communicated to the unfortunate parents, who arrived at the NICU two hours later by public transport. Their faces reflected a mix of desperation and exhaustion. Upon entering the unit, the pain overwhelmed them immediately, and they broke into tears, their sobs echoing down the halls like a ghostly refrain.

The parents approached the tiny body of their baby, lying lifeless in the incubator. Their tears fell onto the small figure as they searched for answers from the medical staff. The compassionate looks of the nurses could offer neither comfort nor certainties. Amid their sobs, the parents implored for a clear explanation, something that could not be provided due to the lack of immediate information.

The hospital, already a place of constant struggles between life and death, seemed gloomier that night. Waiting for the autopsy results felt like an eternity, a time during which the mystery clung to everyone's mind. The NICU, normally a place of fragile hope, had become a space where silent terror seeped into every corner.

Dr. Lucio Vicens, caught between his professionalism and a growing sense of helplessness, could not shake the image of the grayish baby from his mind. Unanswered questions haunted him. Was there something in the hospital, something they couldn't see, that was affecting the most vulnerable patients? The inexplicable death of the baby was just the beginning; he felt it deep within his being.

The NICU team continued with their routine, but a shadow of uncertainty loomed over them. The monitors maintained their somber song, and each beep seemed more sinister than the last. The parents, their faces marked by pain and despair, clung to the promise of answers, while the medical staff grappled with the growing sense that something sinister lurked within the hospital walls.

During those two weeks of waiting, the atmosphere in the NICU grew increasingly tense. The days lengthened and the nights grew darker, filled with murmurs and unintelligible whispers. Every shadow seemed to come to life, and the dark corners of the hospital became places where the mind played cruel tricks.

The certainty that the hospital hid dark secrets strengthened with each passing day. Lucio knew that the autopsy could reveal more than they were looking for, perhaps even a truth that would forever change his perception of life and death. The wait, with its promises of answers and revelations, became a silent torture as the shadow of terror loomed over the NICU, relentless and omnipresent.

Two weeks later, the standard autopsy revealed no specific indications of a cause of death. There were no signs of poisoning with the usual substances nor traces of excessive medication in the bloodstream. The baby's death remained a medical enigma, a piece that didn't fit into the puzzle of his fragile health. In the absence of clear answers, the senior management of the institution was notified.

The management, with its usual pragmatism, would probably not take further action. The police would not be notified because the patient's medical conditions met the minimum criteria for a premature death. However, not everyone in the hospital was convinced by this explanation. Some suspected that something more sinister was happening, though they couldn't pinpoint exactly what.

Amarilis Cintron, for example, maintained a facade of sadness and concern. But beneath that mask, other feelings were hidden. She knew the procedures and the system's weaknesses all too well. She knew how to maneuver in the shadows, how to conceal actions and disguise intentions.

The unfortunate parents of the baby had arrived at the NICU two hours after the death, devastated and exhausted. Their tears, laden with a mix of pain and confusion, found no solace in the vague answers of the medical staff. Amid their sobs, they implored for an explanation that, due to the lack of immediate information, could not be provided.

"What happened? Why did our baby die?" they asked, their voices broken by anguish. The responses were formal and empty, full of technicalities that offered no comfort. They had to wait for the autopsy results, a mandatory procedure in these cases, which would take approximately two weeks.

The hospital, a place of constant struggles between life and death, grew even gloomier that night. Waiting for the autopsy results felt like an eternity, a time during which mystery and suspicion clung to everyone's mind. The NICU, normally a place of fragile hope, had transformed into a space where silent terror infiltrated every corner.

Dr. Lucio Vicens, trapped between his professionalism and a growing sense of helplessness, could not shake the image of the grayish baby from his mind. Unanswered questions haunted him, unsettling him more and more. Was there something in the hospital, something they couldn't see, that was affecting the most vulnerable patients? The inexplicable death of the baby was just the beginning, and Lucio felt it deep within his being.

The NICU team continued with their routine, but a shadow of uncertainty loomed over them. The monitors maintained their somber song, and each beep seemed more sinister than the last. The parents, their faces marked by pain and despair, clung to the promise of answers, while the medical staff grappled with the growing sense that something sinister lurked within the hospital walls.

During those two weeks of waiting, the atmosphere in the NICU grew increasingly tense. The days lengthened and the nights grew darker, filled with murmurs and unintelligible whispers. Every shadow seemed to come to life, and the dark corners of the hospital became places where the mind played cruel tricks.

The certainty that the hospital hid dark secrets strengthened with each passing day. Lucio knew that the autopsy could reveal more than they were looking for, perhaps even a truth that would forever change his perception of life and death. The wait, with its promises of answers and revelations, became a silent torture as the shadow of terror loomed over the NICU, relentless and omnipresent.

But Amarilis, with her innocent appearance, knew the secret was safe for now. She had maneuvered carefully, manipulating both the medications and the emotions of those around her. Within her, a dark satisfaction grew as she watched the uncertainty and fear take hold of the hospital. She was the shadow in the NICU, the presence no one could see, but who controlled every movement from the shadows.

II

In the darkness of the room, a muffled scream broke the nocturnal silence. Little Amarilis sat up in her bed, cold sweat sticking the sheet to her trembling skin. The shadows of the night danced on the walls, as if they were the ghosts of her nightmare following her into reality.

"Mama!" Her voice was a thread, barely audible amidst her sobs.

Within seconds, the door opened with a soft creak and her mother's figure appeared in the doorway, a comforting shadow against the dim hallway light.

"Amarilis, my life, did you have another bad dream?" Her mother quickly approached, sitting on the edge of the bed. She extended her arms, and Amarilis nestled against her, seeking refuge in her warmth.

"Yes, Mama. The monsters... the monsters were everywhere," the child babbled, the words coming out broken by fear.

"Shhhh, it's over now, my heart. They are just dreams; they can't hurt you," her mother murmured, stroking her sweat-drenched hair. "You're here with me, you're safe."

"But they felt real, Mommy, like... like the monster wanted to take me with him," Amarilis's voice trembled as she clung tighter to her mother.

"Dreams sometimes play tricks on us, especially on creative minds like yours. But remember, every time you wake up from a bad dream, I will be here. Nothing and no one can hurt you while I'm by your side."

"Do you promise you won't leave me?" Her wide, fearful eyes sought certainty in her mother's gaze.

"I promise, my love. I will always be with you," her words were a gentle vow in the darkness, a promise meant to be unbreakable.

Amarilis nodded, letting her mother's presence smooth the edges of her fear. Gradually, the warmth and security offered by her mother's arms calmed her, and her eyelids began to grow heavy again.

"Try to sleep, darling. I'll be here, watching over your dreams," her mother said, and kissed her forehead, a guardian against the shadows of the night.

With the comfort of that promise, the five-year-old closed her eyes, breathing more easily. The night was still dark and long, but the proximity of her mother comforted her, a beacon in the storm of her nightmares.

Thus passed those gloomy days in the child's existence, days in which both mother and daughter woke up besieged by the specters of the past, those dark shadows that refused to be forgotten. Neither of them, in their innocence and desire to find some peace, knew that the specter of evil had only multiplied, a sinister echo repeating with each new dawn. Amarilis's mother, once again driven by the impulses of a lonely heart, had fallen prey to the venomous charm of a new love, one tainted by envy and possession disguised as passion.

This new companion, who at first appeared to be a refuge and a promising new beginning, soon revealed his true nature. Beneath the mask of affection lay a jealous and controlling character, a man who saw his loved ones as property rather than beings with free will. Thus, the house that was supposed to be a sanctuary slowly transformed into a prison, and the days were tinged with barely concealed tension, a prelude to coming storms.

Amarilis, with the keen perception of childhood, soon began to feel the change in the air, an electric charge of unspoken omens. Her mother, trying to protect her daughter, wrapped reality in layers of silence and half-truths. However, Amarilis's fear could not be assuaged, and her nights filled with new nightmares, where threatening figures and elongated shadows played leading roles in nocturnal theaters of terror.

In those moments of vulnerability, when the veil of sleep was abruptly torn by the child's muffled scream, her mother would come, her figure a trembling but firm pillar in the dim room. She consoled Amarilis with whispers of love and promises of protection, a ritual both knew by heart but that, each night, seemed to lose some of its consoling power.

Thus, the cycle of day and night continued, a reflection of the duality of hope and despair, an endless loop where past and present intertwined, increasingly indistinguishable from one another in Amarilis's mind and heart. The presence of the new man, far from being a balm, became a constant reminder that sometimes, ghosts are as real as the flesh and bone that house them.

But the fateful days arrived when the new paternal figure in little Amarilis's life became even more frightening than her brute natural father. This man, younger than her mother, was a disturbing presence, a cruel parody of what a protector should be. His gaze, filled with greed, followed her around the house, and the contempt with which he treated her mother was a daily spectacle.

Every night, the house transformed into a horror stage. Her mother's bedroom door remained open, and he, with a perverse smile, ensured that Amarilis could see. He used her mother's body with brutality and disdain, adopting indecent positions, exhibiting a vulgarity the little girl could not fully understand but instinctively sensed as profoundly evil.

"Oh, what a coincidence," he would say in a sugary voice when he saw her in the doorway. "I didn't mean for you to see this, little one. You should be in your bed."

But it was no coincidence. He knew exactly what he was doing. He wanted her to see, to let the horror and confusion claw into her mind like invisible talons. Every night, Amarilis remained petrified, watching the scene with a mixture of fear and repulsion. Her heart pounded, her small body trembled, and terror gripped her soul.

The shadows in the room seemed to come to life, twisting and contorting into grotesque shapes. The flickering light from the hallway cast unsettling silhouettes on the walls, and every whisper, every moan, resonated in her mind like a macabre echo. There was no escape from this constant nightmare, a warped reality that followed her even into her dreams.

Her mother, trapped in her own misery, did not see the look of hatred and resentment that Amarilis directed at the man. She was too consumed by her own sadness, too broken to protect her daughter. Amarilis learned to survive in silence, to hide her emotions and build walls around her heart.

As the days passed, the hatred and desire for revenge grew within her. She knew that someday, somehow, she would have the power to confront that monster and others like him. Little Amarilis, with her stolen innocence, began to plot in silence, her dark thoughts intertwined with the desire for justice.

Every greedy look, every vulgar gesture, was etched into her mind, fueling a darkness that was slowly growing. Inside her, the promise that one day she would be the one in control, who could decide over life and death, became her reason to keep going.

Finally, after years of abuse and torment, Amarilis's mother gathered the courage to leave the stepfather. One night, after a particularly violent argument, where the brute sexually assaulted her, she took Amarilis's hand and, with tears in her eyes and firm determination, fled from the house that had been their prison. They found refuge in a women's shelter, where they began to rebuild their lives, far from the man who had caused them so much pain. This escape marked a turning point in Amarilis's life, but the scars of the past would continue to affect her deeply, shaping her future decisions.

The hospital, with its cold lights and endless hallways, became the perfect setting for her revenge. Amarilis moved through the shadows, always alert, always calculating. She knew that the time of the monsters would come to an end, and she would be the architect of their downfall.

Every time she looked at a vulnerable patient, in extremis, she remembered that man, and a cold smile spread across her face. The terror she had suffered transformed into a powerful force, a fierce determination that no one suspected. In the NICU, Amarilis was not just a nurse; she was a lurking shadow, a presence that controlled the fate of the weakest with terrifying precision.

And so, the cycle of terror continued, but this time, Amarilis was in command, her dark past guiding every one of her movements, every decision made in the dimly lit hospital.

In her preadolescence, Amarilis became a master of avoidance. Every situation that could remind her of the abuse suffered in her childhood was meticulously avoided. Enclosed spaces provoked an insurmountable claustrophobia, and being alone with men who reminded her of her stepfather was something she could not bear. The scars of her past governed her behavior, delineating her interactions and movements as if they were the outlines of a constant nightmare.

When she found herself in a confined space, the air seemed to become thick and suffocating. Amarilis felt as if the walls were closing in on her, crushing her with memories she preferred to keep buried. She avoided elevators, small rooms, and any place where shadows could come to life again and drag her back to the past. At school, she always chose seats next to doors or near windows, ensuring she had an escape route.

Her hypervigilance was evident in her daily life. She overreacted to loud noises, sudden movements, or unexpected touches. A sudden door slam made her jump from her seat, her heart beating wildly as if trying to escape from her chest. Abrupt movements around her made her recoil, and an unexpected touch on her shoulder could cause her to sweat and shake uncontrollably. Her classmates looked at her with curiosity and sometimes with mockery, but Amarilis was beyond caring about their opinions; her only concern was keeping her mind and body under control.

Nights were especially difficult. The silence of the home only amplified her memories. Every creak of the wood, every whisper of the wind against the windows, took her back to those terrifying nights. She slept with the light on and a chair wedged against the door, in an attempt to create a barrier between her and the monsters that still populated her mind.

Amarilis also developed constant vigilance. In any situation, her eyes were always moving, scanning the environment for threats. She learned to identify danger signs before they fully manifested, a skill that, although exhausting, gave her an illusion of safety. This state of perpetual alertness became second nature to her, and although it made her seem distant and reserved, it was her way of staying safe.

Interactions with men were the most difficult. Any man who bore even a slight resemblance to her stepfather filled her with indescribable unease. She avoided male teachers, doctors, even the fathers of her friends. She preferred to always be in the company of women, in whom she found a measure of comfort and safety. If it was inevitable to be in the presence of a man, she kept her distance, her muscles tense and ready to react at the slightest sign of danger.

Amarilis's adolescence was a constant struggle between the desire to lead a normal life and the need to protect herself from a past that never stopped haunting her. Each day was a silent battle, and each victory was only a breath before the next wave of anxiety. However, in the midst of all that darkness, a fierce determination was strengthening. Amarilis vowed that she would never be a victim again, and that vow became the spark that would eventually lead her to take control in the NICU, to be the shadow deciding over life and death, guided by a past that refused to stay buried.

After finishing high school in her hometown, Amarilis moved to the capital to study nursing at the country's leading health training center. Determined to escape the ghosts of her past and find a purpose in her life, she enrolled in a nursing degree with a concentration in pediatrics. The following years were a mix of challenges and discoveries.

At university, Amarilis immersed herself in her studies with an almost obsessive dedication. She spent long hours in the library, memorizing medical terms and learning about the various disorders and treatments affecting children. Her outstanding grades distinguished her as one of the best students in her class, and her natural ability to care for young patients did not go unnoticed.

Despite her talent, Amarilis found no true peace. Her devotion to the children reflected her own suffering. Every time she looked at a sick child, she saw a reflection of her own broken childhood. The innocence of those little beings constantly reminded her that she too had been a victim of circumstances, trapped in a life of abuse and pain.

During her clinical practice, Amarilis excelled in the pediatric unit. Her patience and tenderness with the young patients earned her the respect of her colleagues and the admiration of the parents. However, behind that facade of compassion and professionalism, her mind was a battlefield. Every time she held the hand of a sick child, the shadow of her past loomed over her, reminding her of nights of terror and days of despair.

The nights in her small apartment in the capital were lonely and plagued with disturbing memories. The echo of her stepfather's screams and the sight of her mother suffering still haunted her. She slept with the light on, trying to ward off the shadows that seemed to come to life in the darkness. Often, she found herself crying silently, clutching a pillow that could offer no comfort.

Work in the pediatric unit provided her with a kind of redemption. Amarilis clung to the idea that by caring for the children, she was protecting her younger self, the defenseless girl who had no one to defend her. However, that same devotion began to distort. She started to see the fragility of life not only as something to be protected but also as something that could be released from suffering.

The pressure and darkness of her mind began to manifest in subtle ways. She became more reserved, her eyes always vigilant, constantly scanning her surroundings for invisible threats. She often caught herself imagining scenarios where she could permanently relieve the children's pain, her thoughts growing darker and darker.

Graduation came with honors, and Amarilis accepted a position at the prestigious National Pediatric Hospital. Her colleagues admired her dedication and skills, but no one knew the true storm that raged within her. Amarilis settled into her new job, determined to do everything possible to help the children, even though her concept of help was becoming dangerously ambiguous.

In the NICU, Nurse Amarilis Cintron found the perfect place to hide her inner demons behind a mask of compassion and professionalism. As the monitors beeped and the lives of the little ones hung by a thread, she moved with the precision and coldness of someone who deeply understood pain and despair. The shadow of her past continued to haunt her, guiding her actions and decisions in a macabre dance between life and death.

When she was a nursing student, Amarilis fortuitously met a young man named Esteban Fuertes. Esteban, who was studying for a PhD in chemistry, spent his time in the laboratory like a mouse, always immersed in his research. Unlike Amarilis, who was reserved and cautious, Esteban was communicative, intelligent, and handsome. He came from Colombia as part of a student exchange program to complete his PhD at the same university where Amarilis was studying.

One day, while she was in the nursing faculty cafeteria, Esteban approached her with an open smile and a friendly attitude.

"Hello, can I buy you a coffee?" he said for the first time, his voice full of confidence.

Students frequented these places in search of the prettiest and youngest girls on campus, and Esteban was no exception. When their eyes met directly, something ignited within both of them. Amarilis, more apprehensive than Esteban, looked away first. She flatly rejected the suggestion of sharing a cup of coffee with him, her instinct for self-preservation at the forefront. But Esteban was not discouraged. He knew it was worth insisting, and like a drop that repeatedly falls on a stone until it leaves a dent, he persisted in his attempt to get to know her.

The third time was the charm, and Amarilis finally agreed to have a coffee with him. It was during that conversation that Esteban mentioned his work in the chemistry lab, and Amarilis's interest notably increased. There was something about Esteban's passion for his work that sparked Amarilis's curiosity, and she found herself listening intently as he explained his research.

Esteban told her that he had been sent by the Colombian military government to study the processing of ricin, a highly toxic substance that had previously been used as a biological weapon. His job was to derive enough ricin and, at the same time, develop an antidote for its poisoning. This combination of danger and noble purpose resonated deeply with Amarilis, awakening in her a mix of admiration and a dark interest.

"It's fascinating, though dangerous," said Amarilis, her eyes shining with a mix of curiosity and something deeper that even she could not fully identify.

Esteban nodded; his enthusiasm evident. "Yes, it's a challenge, but I think it's important. If we manage to develop an effective antidote, we could save many lives in the event of a bioterrorist attack."

Esteban's words ignited a spark in Amarilis's mind. Here was a man not only passionate about his work but also dedicated to protecting others from an invisible but deadly danger. In her mind, an idea began to take shape, a possibility of how she could use this knowledge for her own dark and distorted purposes of "mercy."

The meetings in the cafeteria became more frequent, and each conversation with Esteban turned into a valuable lesson. Amarilis absorbed the information like a sponge, learning about the chemistry behind ricin, its lethal effects, and the difficulties in developing an antidote. Esteban, suspecting nothing, generously shared his knowledge, happy to have someone interested in his work.

As their relationship progressed, Esteban became a beacon of light in Amarilis's life, a connection she had never experienced before. However, the shadow of her past and the distortion of her mind continued to lurk, and although she admired Esteban, she also saw in his knowledge a potential tool for her own purposes.

Amarilis knew she had to be cautious. The information she was obtaining from Esteban could be dangerous in the wrong hands, and she struggled between genuine admiration for him and the dark desire to use what she was learning. Thus, each cup of coffee, each conversation, became a delicate dance between light and shadow, as Amarilis continued her path toward an uncertain future, laden with both redemptive and destructive possibilities.

III

Three months after the inexplicable death of the newborn, another fatal event shook the NICU. Although patients in the unit frequently died due to prematurity and severe medical conditions, this particular case defied all scientific explanation. The affected baby was a premature infant of twenty-eight weeks gestation who had been born weighing 875 grams with a defect called omphalocele. This defect was immense, and the baby had been delivered by cesarean section.

Dr. Lucio Vicens, the lead surgeon, had determined that the baby needed a sclerosing agent on the defect's covering so that the skin would grow and protect the membrane covering the intestines. The management plan was to wait until the baby was between two and three years old to repair the remaining abdominal hernia. This way, the baby could gain weight, feed properly, and avoid an early surgical procedure, considering that the liver was also part of the defect.

Two weeks had passed since the tiny newborn's birth. The defect was as large as the baby's head, deeply affecting Amarilis every time she attended to him. She couldn't understand how a baby in that condition could survive. She only saw the baby's suffering and that of his parents, trapped in a painful crossroads due to the congenital defect and low weight.

"How is the baby with omphalocele doing, Miss Cintron?" asked Dr. Lucio Vicens one morning during his rounds.

While examining the congenital defect and the effect of the sclerosing agents on the membrane, Nurse Cintron ventured to comment and question:

"He looks stable, but I don't think he's going to survive with that defect. What do you think, doctor?"

"Of course, he's going to survive. We're not doing anything invasive, just feeding him to gain weight and applying Silvadene so the skin will grow. Do you see those darker areas? That's skin growing over the membrane," explained Dr. Vicens.

"Sure, I understand, doctor, but this is going to take a long time, and those parents are suffering..." said Amarilis with a mix of compassion and doubt.

"I understand, Amarilis, you have a beautiful heart, but this is the plan of action. When he gains at least two kilos of weight and the new skin covers the defect, we can discharge him," the doctor replied with firmness and empathy.

"I trust you, doctor," murmured Amarilis, though inside she felt confused.

"Thank you. Now let's move on to this other case," said Dr. Vicens as he moved from incubator to incubator, superficially examining the surgical cases and reviewing the most recent vital signs and lab data on the computers before slipping out the door.

Amarilis stayed behind, reflecting on what the doctor had said. More so, the doctor's attitude reminded her unsettlingly of her stepfather, the man who had disrupted her early years and left lasting traumas. Her mind began to wander, questioning whether the baby's and his parents' suffering was worth the prolonged treatment. The shadow of her past darkened her perception of the present, and a disquieting sense of déjà vu took hold of her.

The constant suffering, she observed in the NICU stirred painful and distorted memories of her own childhood, strengthening her conviction that freeing these little beings from pain could be an act of compassion, a twisted form of mercy that only she understood.

For the second time that year, the monitors of the baby with the abdominal wall defect went haywire, emitting alarms indicating the development of a cardiac arrhythmia known as ventricular fibrillation. The medical staff reacted immediately, intubating the patient and starting cardiopulmonary resuscitation. For forty-five minutes, the team worked tirelessly, trying to stabilize the tiny patient. Despite their efforts, the baby was declared dead at 2:20 pm.

Dr. Lucio Vicens was at the institution giving a lecture to medical students when he received a notification on his WhatsApp app about the fatal event. The news left him cold. He had left the baby stable that very morning, tolerating breast milk without apparent complications. After finishing the lecture, he rushed to the neonatal intensive care unit to find out what had happened.

Upon arriving at the NICU, the atmosphere was heavy and tense. The monitors emitted their usual beeps, but a palpable sadness hung over the staff. Amarilis, with a deeply sad expression on her face, approached Dr. Lucio Vicens to inform him of the details.

"What happened with the baby?" asked Lucio, his voice laden with concern and exhaustion.

"Doctor, the monitors detected ventricular fibrillation. We initiated resuscitation immediately and worked for forty-five minutes, but we couldn't save him," replied Amarilis, her eyes avoiding direct contact.

Lucio walked over to the empty incubator, his thoughts filled with confusion and frustration. He mentally retraced the steps he had taken, looking for any signs he might have missed.

"We left him stable this morning. He was tolerating breast milk without problems. I don't understand what could have gone wrong so suddenly," he murmured to himself, though Amarilis could hear him clearly.

The nurse nodded, sharing the doctor's confusion. However, within her, a whirlwind of emotions and dark thoughts swirled. Although she displayed compassion and professionalism, her mind was in a constant battle between appearance and her hidden actions.

"We'll conduct a thorough review of the chart and the monitors. We need to understand what happened," said Lucio, trying to regain his composure. Perhaps the baby aspirated food massively, he speculated.

As he headed to review the records, the shadow of Amarilis's past continued to haunt her, feeding her distorted thoughts about compassion and relieving suffering. The echo of her childhood traumas resonated with every step, reminding her that, in her twisted way, she believed she was doing the right thing.

Like a repeated movie, the established protocol for an unjustifiable medical death was followed. The process began with a standard autopsy, followed by a thorough toxicological analysis to detect the most common substances, including those the patient received by any existing means.

The autopsy room at the National Pediatric Hospital was illuminated with cold, bright lights that accentuated the clinical and dispassionate atmosphere of the place. The forensic pathologists, dressed in white coats and latex gloves, worked with meticulous precision. The tiny body of the baby, now lifeless, lay on the stainless-steel table, while the surgical instruments gleamed, ready to be used.

Dr. Lucio Vicens watched from the observation window, his face reflecting a mix of sadness and determination. He had seen too many unexplained deaths in the NICU and was determined to find answers. Every step of the protocol was followed rigorously: the opening of the body, the meticulous inspection of the organs, the collection of blood and tissue samples for toxicological analysis.

Meanwhile, Amarilis Cintron continued with her daily routine, but something in her behavior had changed. Although she maintained her facade of professionalism, those who knew her well noticed a slight tremor in her hands and a distant look in her eyes. Inside her, a storm of emotions and dark thoughts raged, reminding her of her own scars and traumas.

The baby's parents arrived immediately at the NICU, their faces marked by despair and pain. They collapsed to the floor, crying inconsolably over the loss of their only child. It was a tragic moment for a family that had undergone numerous fertility treatments for a long time, as they could not have children due to the father's oligospermia. A direct implantation of a fertilized egg in the laboratory with the mother's oocytes and the few sperm from the father had produced the baby who had just died.

The sight of the devastated parents struck deeply into Amarilis's heart. Their tears and screams echoed through the NICU hallways, and the intensity of their pain was palpable. She remembered her own silent screams from her childhood, and a dark empathy mixed with her already distorted view of mercy.

The toxicology lab received the samples and began the analysis process. The technicians worked with sophisticated machines, searching for traces of any substance that could have caused the baby's death. The list included everything from common medications to exotic toxins, anything that could shed light on what had happened.

Days later, the results came back: no unusual substances were found in the baby's system. The cause of death remained a mystery, and the baby had not aspirated food. This only increased the frustration and confusion among the hospital staff. The shadow of doubt began to loom over the NICU, and murmurs of concern spread among the doctors and nurses.

Dr. Vicens, dissatisfied with the results, decided that additional tests were necessary. He ordered a deeper analysis, including tests to detect less common and more difficult-to-identify compounds. He knew something was wrong and would not rest until he discovered what it was.

Meanwhile, Amarilis struggled internally. She knew that continuing her actions was becoming increasingly risky, but the urge to free the little ones from suffering persisted. The duality of her being, divided between the compassionate nurse and the dark angel of death, consumed her slowly.

Each death was a reminder of her own powerlessness and the need to exert control in a world that had taken everything from her. Amarilis moved like a shadow through the hospital hallways, her thoughts growing darker and more distorted. The NICU, a place of hope and struggle for life, became the stage for her macabre theater of misunderstood mercy.

The oppressive silence of the night in the hospital was broken only by the beeping of monitors and the whispers of the staff, unaware of the sinister presence lurking among them. Amarilis, with a disturbing calm, continued her routine, always watching, always waiting for the right moment to act. She knew that the time for secrets was coming to an end and that the truth, however dark, would eventually come to light.

The sight of the inconsolable parents, whose baby was the result of arduous fertility treatment, only strengthened her twisted conviction. She believed she was helping these families, freeing them from a suffering she knew all too well. While the parents wept, Amarilis watched from the shadows, her heart divided between compassion and darkness.

The unit's staff became reserved about what was happening. They looked at each other with suspicion, searching for a possible culprit. Trust had eroded, and every action was observed with suspicion. Everything was documented with obsessive precision. They knew it was only a matter of time before something similar happened again, and they were on the lookout, determined to discover what was going on.

The atmosphere in the NICU was tense, almost palpable. Nurses and doctors, who had once worked in harmony, now performed their tasks with extreme caution. Conversations had been reduced to the strictly necessary, and the exchange of glances was frequent, full of suspicion. Every procedure, every medication administered, was carefully noted and reviewed, looking for any sign of irregularity.

Amarilis moved among them, maintaining her facade of professionalism and compassion. But inside her, the tension was growing. She knew that the atmosphere of suspicion made her actions increasingly risky. However, the urge to continue her macabre plan of "mercy" was stronger. She watched her colleagues with a mix of calculated calm and growing paranoia.

Every shift in the NICU was like walking a tightrope. The monitors emitted their constant beeps, the fluorescent lights illuminated the tired and watchful faces of the staff. Shift change meetings had turned into meticulous analysis sessions, where every detail of the past hours was examined with a fine-tooth comb. Dr. Lucio Vicens, feeling the increasing pressure, called a meeting with all the staff to address the situation.

"I understand that we are all worried and that trust has been affected," began Dr. Vicens, his voice firm but with a note of exhaustion. "But we must remain calm and follow protocols more rigorously than ever. We cannot let fear paralyze us."

The doctor's words resonated in the room but did not entirely dispel the cloud of suspicion. Amarilis watched from a corner, her mind working feverishly to ensure that her next actions would be flawless, leaving no traces that could incriminate her. She knew that one misstep could be her undoing, but her determination was unwavering.

The staff, meanwhile, continued their vigilance, noting every detail and observing every movement. Nights were especially difficult when the hospital's silence became oppressive, and every shadow seemed to come to life. Suspicions not only hung over the NICU staff but also over the procedures and technology they used. Every mistake, no matter how small, was magnified under the lens of distrust.

Amarilis, aware that she was under constant scrutiny, adjusted her strategy. She became even more meticulous, carefully tending to every detail of her actions. She knew she had to maintain her impeccable facade while continuing her disturbing mission of "mercy." The line between her compassion and her darkness blurred more and more, fed by the memories of her own suffering and the twisted belief that she was doing the right thing.

The atmosphere in the NICU remained tense, but Amarilis knew that as long as she could maintain control, her secret would remain safe. The staff was on alert, but so was she, always one step ahead, always ready to act when the moment was right.

The tension continued to build, and the hospital, a place of hope and healing, had become a scene of suspicion and fear. With each passing day, the shadow of the truth loomed closer, and Amarilis knew that the conclusion was drawing nearer, inevitable, and laden with consequences.

For its part, the senior management of the institution's executive committee met to determine the appropriate course of action regarding what was happening. They knew it was imperative to inform the relevant authorities and open a criminal investigation confidentially to avoid affecting the institution's image in the community.

The meeting was held in a conference room isolated from the usual bustle of the hospital. The serious and concerned expressions of the executives reflected the gravity of the situation. The hospital's executive director, with a furrowed brow, initiated the conversation:

"We must act quickly and discreetly. We cannot allow these unexplained deaths to continue without acting," he said, his voice firm but full of concern.

"I agree," responded one of the committee members. "But we must be extremely careful. If the news leaks, we could face a crisis of confidence with the community and a wave of panic among the parents of the children hospitalized here."

It was decided that the best strategy was to initiate an internal investigation first, while preparing to contact the health authorities and eventually the police. Confidentiality was crucial; any hint of negligence or crime had to be handled with the utmost discretion.

"We need to ensure that all evidence and records are thoroughly reviewed," added another executive. "Nothing can be left to chance. We must find the cause of these deaths, whatever it may be."

The directive began to outline an action plan. A specialized team was designated to review all the records of the deceased babies, from their medical histories to medication logs and security camera recordings in the NICU. Every detail would be thoroughly examined.

Meanwhile, Amarilis continued with her routine, seemingly unaware of the growing storm. However, she knew that time was running out. The presence of senior management in the NICU and the inquisitive looks from her colleagues indicated that the situation was becoming unsustainable.

The internal investigation team began their work immediately. Each reviewed file was a piece of the puzzle they were trying to assemble. Autopsies became more detailed, and additional toxicological analyses were requested. The employees' movements were monitored more rigorously, and any suspicious behavior was reported and evaluated.

The tension in the NICU grew daily. Murmurs and furtive glances intensified. The staff knew that something dark was happening, and the pressure from senior management only increased the general nervousness.

"We cannot allow this to continue in the shadows," said the director in one of the follow-up meetings. "If someone is harming our patients, we will find them and bring them to justice."

The hospital's image was at stake, and senior management knew it. Every decision had to be made with precision and care to protect the institution and, more importantly, the vulnerable young patients.

Amarilis, meanwhile, perfected her mask of professionalism and compassion. She knew her days of freedom to act were limited, but her conviction remained firm. In her mind, every action was justified by a twisted sense of mercy. However, the increasing surveillance and the feeling that the net was tightening began to affect her.

Senior management, committed to solving the mystery and stopping the wave of unexplained deaths, moved with determination. They knew that the truth, however painful, had to come to light and that it was their responsibility to protect the most vulnerable under their care.

The hospital, a place of hope and healing, had become an invisible battleground where trust, ethics, and safety were at stake. The shadow of the truth loomed closer, and everyone knew that the conclusion was drawing nearer, inevitable and loaded with consequences.

Reviewing the files of the past ten years, the internal investigation team discovered a disturbing pattern: eight additional neonatal deaths in the past five years that lacked a coherent medical explanation. This revelation deepened the mystery and increased the urgency of the situation.

Each reviewed file told a similar story. Neonates who initially seemed stable but suddenly suffered fatal complications without an apparent cause. The deaths, although spaced out over time, showed patterns that had previously gone unnoticed. The detailed review of these cases revealed that, in many of them, the records were meticulous, but something didn't add up. The causes of death were ambiguous, and the autopsies did not yield conclusive results.

Senior management met again, now with an even greater sense of urgency. The hospital director, with a grave expression, opened the meeting:

"We cannot ignore this. Eight additional deaths, all without a coherent medical explanation. We have to assume that we are facing a serious and potentially criminal problem," he said, looking at the committee members.

One of the executives, specialized in epidemiology, spoke up: "These patterns are too consistent to be coincidences. We need to delve into each case, review every detail, and consider the possibility that someone within our institution is involved in these events."

It was decided that, in addition to the internal investigation, it was imperative to contact the police authorities. Confidentiality remained crucial, but the severity of the situation required the intervention of experts in criminology and external forensic medicine.

Meanwhile, in the NICU, the atmosphere of suspicion and tension continued to increase. The staff, aware of the exhaustive review of the records and the growing surveillance, worked under constant pressure. Amarilis, although external to the decisions of senior management, felt the weight of inquisitive looks and the charged environment.

The external forensic team arrived at the hospital to collaborate with the investigation. Their focus was on the similarities between the cases, looking for any indication that could point to a specific modus operandi. They analyzed medical histories, the circumstances of the deaths, and the records of administered medications. Every detail, no matter how insignificant it seemed, was investigated.

Amarilis moved with heightened caution. She knew that any mistake could expose her. Every time the investigators approached to review a file or asked about procedures, her heart pounded. The pressure was immense, but her determination remained unshakable. In her mind, she continued to justify her actions as acts of mercy, although she knew that the truth was dangerously close to being discovered.

The review of old records revealed more disturbing details. In several cases, it was observed that the babies had shown improvement before suddenly succumbing to inexplicable complications. The shift logs indicated that Amarilis had been present at many of these critical moments, a detail that did not go unnoticed by the investigators.

Dr. Lucio Vicens, informed of the preliminary findings, began to connect the dots. His analytical mind and medical experience led him to suspect that something sinister was behind the deaths. His confidence in Amarilis wavered, and although he did not want to believe it, the clues began to point in an alarming direction.

Senior management, aware of the growing evidence, intensified the surveillance and monitoring of the staff. Additional cameras were installed, and stricter protocols were implemented for handling medications and accessing patients. The NICU became a place of constant supervision, where every movement was observed and recorded.

IV

It was time to alert the police authorities. The case was assigned to an expert in crimes within hospital institutions and a doctor of pediatrics, Leticia Moran. Dr. Moran, known for her precision and determination, was the ideal person to handle this complex and disturbing case.

She was an imposing woman, standing close to six feet tall and weighing 155 pounds, giving her a notable physical presence. Her brown eyes were penetrating, and her smile, which seemed to suggest she knew what one was thinking, completed her impressive résumé. This ability to read people and anticipate their moves made her a formidable investigator.

She dressed impeccably. She wore a shirt, tie, and pants from a sophisticated brand, complemented by Christian Louboutin shoes with red soles. Everything about her appearance indicated that money flowed easily in her environment.

Leticia had solved several crimes in hospital and academic institutions with surprising precision. Her reputation as an expert in unraveling the most complex cases preceded her, and her meticulous and detailed approach made her feared and respected in equal measure.

In addition, Leticia was a lesbian and lived with a federal court judge, which gave her an advantage in any investigation, as she could gather the necessary resources in time. This relationship provided her with privileged access to information and legal support, making her an even more powerful force in her field.

Leticia Moran was not only a brilliant investigator but also a woman with a strong sense of justice and unwavering determination. Every case she took on was a personal mission, and she did not rest until the truth came to light. Her combination of academic skills and practical experience made her the ideal candidate to tackle the disturbing events in the NICU.

Leticia Moran arrived at the hospital with the efficiency and professionalism that characterized her. With a firm demeanor and a keen gaze, she immediately met with senior management and the internal investigation team. Her experience in both pediatrics and investigating hospital crimes made her particularly suited to unravel the mystery surrounding the unexplained deaths in the NICU.

"Thank you for your cooperation and discretion in this delicate matter," Leticia said as she addressed the conference room. "I have reviewed the preliminary reports and am aware of the eight additional deaths in the last five years. My goal is to identify any patterns or irregularities that will lead us to an explanation."

Dr. Moran began by meticulously reviewing each file, cross-referencing information with personnel records and work shifts. She immediately noticed that Amarilis Cintron had been present at many, if not all, of the critical moments of the deaths. This pattern could not be a mere coincidence.

"We need to conduct thorough interviews with all NICU staff," ordered Leticia. "I want to know their routines, any unusual behavior, and any recent changes in their professional or personal lives."

The NICU staff were summoned one by one to be questioned by Dr. Moran and her team. The questions were meticulous, delving into their movements during shifts, their relationships with patients and colleagues, and any strange observations they might have made. Amarilis, like the others, was interviewed. She maintained her composure, answering with the same professionalism that had always characterized her.

"I have worked here for five years, always putting the welfare of the babies as my priority," said Amarilis with a firm but serene voice. "These deaths affect me deeply, and I will do everything I can to help with the investigation," she added.

Despite her apparent sincerity, Leticia noticed a calculated coldness in her responses. There was something in the way Amarilis spoke about the babies and their suffering that didn't quite fit. Dr. Moran knew she had to proceed cautiously but without wasting time.

Simultaneously, Leticia reviewed all medication records, security cameras, and previous autopsy reports. Every detail was crucial to understanding the full picture. She found inconsistencies in the medication logs and observed behavior patterns that indicated possible manipulation.

Dr. Moran also worked closely with Dr. Lucio Vicens, who, despite his own confusion and pain, provided valuable information about the cases. Together, they began to build a timeline and map out the connections between the deaths.

"Dr. Lucio, I need you to tell me more about Amarilis," requested Leticia. "Anything, no matter how small, could be crucial."

"Amarilis has always been a dedicated nurse," responded Lucio, his voice laden with doubt. "But in retrospect, I've noticed that she was present at critical moments in several cases. I don't want to make unfounded accusations, but something doesn't seem right."

With this information, Leticia intensified surveillance on Amarilis. Additional cameras were installed, and existing recordings were meticulously reviewed. Every interaction Amarilis had with patients and medications was monitored.

The net was closing slowly. Leticia Moran knew she was getting closer to the truth, a dark and disturbing truth that threatened to unravel not only the professionalism of a nurse but also the trust the hospital had built over the years.

Amid this growing tension, Amarilis continued her routine, increasingly aware that her past actions were about to catch up with her. Senior management, the staff, and now the police were all united in a common goal: to uncover the truth and protect the most vulnerable patients.

The cases of merciful euthanasia suddenly decreased. There was no doubt that the perpetrator of the crimes was on alert. The imposing presence of Leticia Moran had made a significant impact. It was only a matter of time before the killer was unmasked.

During this period of tense calm, the NICU seemed to breathe a little more easily. The monitors continued their regular beeping, and medical care proceeded without interruption, but a sense of constant vigilance permeated the environment. Employees were more cautious in their interactions, aware that every move was being watched.

Leticia, with her incisive gaze and analytical mind, maintained rigorous surveillance. Her presence in the hallways and active participation in staff meetings infused a mix of respect and fear. Her questions were precise, and her meticulous inspections made it clear that she would not be easily deceived.

The nurses and doctors, though committed to their work, could not help but feel the pressure of being under constant scrutiny. The forced calm felt fragile, as if it could break at any moment. However, the sense of security increased with the certainty that Leticia was there to protect the most vulnerable.

Amarilis, despite her skill in hiding her true intentions, felt the growing tension. She knew that any mistake, no matter how small, could lead to her discovery. Her routine became even more precise, her behavior more controlled, as she tried to avoid raising suspicions.

Each day, Leticia reviewed medication records, cross-referenced information from security cameras, and interviewed staff. Her goal was clear: find patterns, detect inconsistencies, and unmask the culprit. She knew that the killer, whoever it was, must be feeling the pressure of her presence.

The hospital, though in a temporary truce, remained a silent battlefield. The shadow of previous crimes still hung heavy, and everyone knew that the danger had not completely passed. Leticia Morán's determination was a beacon in that darkness, and her ability to unravel the most complex cases was the hope for justice for the small lives lost.

Leticia knew it was only a matter of time. The killer might have reduced their activities, but they could not hide forever. With each passing day, she got closer to uncovering the truth. The calm that had descended over the NICU was precarious, and Leticia was ready to act at the exact moment.

In this atmosphere of waiting and vigilance, the NICU continued its work. The presence of Leticia Moran, with her combination of intellect and authority, had shifted the balance. The killer knew that time was running out, and Leticia was determined not to rest until justice prevailed.

The feeling that nothing was happening produced a complacency in human beings that dispels doubt, leading them to believe that everything has passed when, in reality, it is just about to begin.

In the NICU, this complacency began to slowly settle among the staff. The reduction in cases of merciful euthanasia and the apparent calm under Leticia Moran's surveillance brought a sigh of relief among the doctors and nurses. However, this tranquility was deceptive. The lack of recent incidents made them lower their guard, thinking the danger had passed.

Amarilis, who had perfected her facade of professionalism, watched this change with a mix of interest and caution. She knew that the real storm had not yet arrived and that her colleagues' complacency could be her ally. The shadow of her past actions remained but hidden under the appearance of normalcy that everyone had begun to accept.

Leticia Moran, with her keen perception, was not fooled by this superficial calm. She knew well that the sense of security could be a dangerous trap. She continued her work with the same intensity, reviewing files, interviewing staff, and analyzing every detail for inconsistencies. Her intuition told her that the killer was just waiting for the right moment to strike again.

The staff, on the other hand, began to relax, laughing a little more in the hallways and regaining some of the lost camaraderie. But this peace was fragile, and Leticia knew it. She had seen too many cases where the criminal took advantage of complacency to strike again.

The atmosphere in the NICU was a mix of relief and latent tension. Surveillance had increased, but the perception that the danger had passed grew stronger. Amarilis, with her ability to remain invisible among her colleagues, watched and waited. She knew that patience was her best ally and that any misstep on her part could crumble her meticulous facade.

Then, Leticia decided to increase the pressure. She called a meeting with all the NICU staff, where she reiterated the importance of not letting their guard down and maintaining surveillance protocols at the highest level. Her firm presence and incisive speech reminded everyone that the case was still open, and that danger could resurface at any moment.

"We must not let this calm deceive us," said Leticia, her gaze sweeping across each of the attendees. "The absence of recent incidents does not mean we have eliminated the threat. We must be more vigilant than ever."

The meeting had the desired effect. The sense of complacency began to dissipate, replaced by renewed vigilance. The staff understood that the tranquility could be the prelude to a new attempt by the killer, and the shadow of doubt settled back among them.

Amarilis, aware of the change in the atmosphere, adjusted her plans. She knew that Leticia would not stop until she found the truth and that her own margin for error was narrowing more and more. However, her conviction that her actions were a form of mercy continued to drive her. She was ready to act when the time was right.

The feeling that nothing happens is deceptive. In the NICU, under the appearance of normalcy, tension continued to grow. The real battle between justice and crime, between calm and storm, was just beginning. Leticia Moran, with her tireless pursuit of the truth, was prepared to face it, and Amarilis, in the shadow of her actions, awaited the outcome of this unsettling game of shadows.

V

The relationship between Amarilis and Esteban grew among books, exams, and studies. What began as a simple exchange of words in the faculty cafeteria transformed into a deep connection, fueled by long hours of study and endless conversations about their respective disciplines. Both found in each other a stimulating and comforting companionship amid the arduous academic pace.

Esteban, with his brilliant intelligence and passion for chemistry, became a pillar of support for Amarilis. Their days were filled with discussions about scientific theories, exchanges of notes, and mutual support during exams. Esteban admired Amarilis's dedication and empathy toward her patients, while Amarilis was inspired by Esteban's inquisitive mind and determination in his research on ricin.

Afternoons in the library were a shared ritual. Sitting together at a table surrounded by books and notes, their hands would casually brush against each other while they searched for information on their laptops. In those moments, the campus bustle faded away, and the world seemed to shrink to the whispers and murmurs of their conversations. Esteban often helped Amarilis understand complex chemistry concepts, while she offered him a clinical and human perspective on the cases they studied.

One of those days, after hours of studying, Esteban decided to open up more to Amarilis. He knew there was something dark and painful in her past, something that made her keep an emotional barrier, but he wanted her to know she could trust him.

"Amarilis, I know you've been through difficult things," Esteban said, his voice soft and sincere. "I want you to know you can count on me for anything. You don't have to carry it all alone."

Amarilis looked at him, her eyes reflecting a mix of surprise and gratitude. She had kept her pain hidden for so long that the idea of sharing it with someone both scared and comforted her.

"Thank you, Esteban," she replied, her voice breaking with emotion. "It's hard to talk about certain things, but I appreciate your support more than you can imagine."

As their relationship deepened, Esteban also began to share more about his own life. He talked about his family in Colombia, his aspirations, and the challenges he had faced to get where he was. These confessions created an even stronger bond between them, based on trust and mutual understanding.

However, amid this growing connection, Amarilis could not ignore the dark impulse that had accompanied her since childhood. Despite her best efforts to find normalcy and happiness with Esteban, the memories of her stepfather and the pain she had suffered continued to haunt her. These ghosts from the past intertwined with her present life, distorting her perception of mercy and compassion.

Esteban, though unaware of the darker details of Amarilis's thoughts, could sense that there was something deeper she had not yet shared. He decided to be patient, convinced that in time, she would open up completely.

In the lab, Esteban continued his research on ricin, sometimes with Amarilis by his side, observing and learning. The experiments and discoveries they made together not only strengthened their professional relationship but also brought them closer on a personal level. Amarilis, fascinated by Esteban's knowledge, absorbed every detail, aware of how that information could apply to her dark inner world.

The relationship between Amarilis and Esteban was a refuge amid their busy lives, a place where they could find comfort and understanding. However, while love and trust flourished, the shadow of Amarilis's past actions and her twisted view of mercy continued to loom, threatening to darken the light they had found together.

Esteban had an apartment near the campus where he studied. It was a small space with one bedroom and one bathroom that he rented for the modest sum of 158,000 pesos per month. Located just half a mile away, this apartment complex was the refuge of hundreds of students of medicine, public health, physical therapy, nursing, and pharmacy. Affordable and nearby, it provided the perfect place for students to focus on their studies without worrying about long commutes.

One night, Esteban decided to invite Amarilis to stay overnight at his apartment. She accepted the invitation with a mix of curiosity and nervousness. Apartment 913, where Esteban lived, faced the mountains, offering a view that provided a breath of tranquility amid the academic hustle.

The apartment was modest but cozy. Textbooks and notes were scattered on a small table, and the walls were adorned with posters of molecules and scientific charts. The atmosphere of study and dedication resonated with the life they both shared.

That night, after a simple dinner and a few hours of study, the conversation between Esteban and Amarilis became more personal. They talked about their dreams, their fears, and the experiences that had shaped them. The connection between them grew stronger with each shared word.

As the night progressed, Esteban took Amarilis's hand, gently guiding her to the small mattress on the floor that served as a bed. The intimacy of the moment was palpable. Amarilis, feeling a mix of intense emotions, let herself be carried away by the warmth and security Esteban provided.

In that encounter in apartment 913, Amarilis shed the veil of her puberty. The physical closeness mingled with the emotional connection they had built, creating a moment of vulnerability and deep union. From the window, the mountains watched silently, witnessing an important milestone in Amarilis's life.

The relationship between them solidified even more after that night. Esteban's apartment became their shared refuge, a place where they could escape academic stress and find comfort in each other's company. Esteban, with his tenderness and understanding, helped Amarilis navigate the complex feelings that arose within her.

However, as their relationship flourished, the ghosts of Amarilis's past did not disappear. The scars of her childhood and the dark impulses she had developed remained, lurking in the corners of her mind. Despite the happiness she found with Esteban, the duality of her being kept her in a constant internal struggle.

Apartment 913, with its view of the mountains and its atmosphere of study and love, became a symbol of hope and challenge in Amarilis's life. Here, alongside Esteban, she experienced moments of genuine connection and happiness, but also faced the memories and emotions that haunted her.

The relationship with Esteban offered her a semblance of normalcy and hope. Each day they spent together; Amarilis found more reasons to fight against the dark thoughts that plagued her. However, the complexity of her psyche and her distorted perception of mercy remained a part of her, waiting for the moment to resurface.

The path they traveled was full of challenges and discoveries, and although the shadow of past traumas remained present, Amarilis found in Esteban a reason to believe in a brighter future. But the balance between their love and her dark impulses would be a constant battle, one that would define her life and the decisions she would make in the future.

Amarilis meticulously learned the molecular structure of ricin, a deadly toxin that Esteban was working on producing with the goal of finding a competitive blocker and developing an efficient antidote. Esteban's dedication to this research fascinated her and, at the same time, awakened a dark interest within her.

Ricin is a toxic protein found naturally in castor beans (Ricinus communis). It is extremely lethal even in small doses and can act quickly to cause death. If injected into the bloodstream, ricin interferes with protein synthesis in cells by inhibiting ribosomes, leading to cell death. The physiological effects on humans include intense pain at the injection site, fever, nausea, and vomiting, followed by multiple organ failure. Within hours, vital organs begin to fail due to the lack of essential proteins, and without treatment, exposure to ricin is generally fatal. Symptoms progress rapidly from severe weakness and lethargy to seizures, internal bleeding, and eventually, death.

As Amarilis delved deeper into her studies on ricin, she understood the lethality of this molecule and the complexity of developing an effective antidote. Her fascination with Esteban's work grew, not only for the possibility of saving lives but also for the destructive power this toxin possessed.

"What would happen if you mixed ricin with epinephrine, Esteban?" Amarilis managed to ask one day in the laboratory.

Esteban, with an air of majestic knowledge, responded to her strange question:

"Well, that would be triply lethal because it would affect the coronary arteries and the myocardium, inhibiting the ribosomes in the cells and preventing them from recovering," he said. He paused to make sure Amarilis understood the gravity of what he was explaining, then continued:

"With one milligram of both injected into a vein, you can end a human life without leaving significant traces," Esteban concluded, his words resonating in the laboratory air.

Amarilis absorbed the information with a mix of fascination and dismay. The combination of epinephrine, which increased heart rate and blood pressure, with ricin, which halted protein synthesis, would be lethal. The epinephrine would cause an overload on the cardiovascular system, while the ricin would destroy vital cells, leading to multi-organ failure.

Esteban, unaware of Amarilis's dark thoughts, immersed himself back into his experiments, satisfied to have shared his knowledge. Amarilis, on the other hand, felt her mind filling with disturbing possibilities, a duality between her love for Esteban and the dark impulses lurking within her.

"How long does ricin remain effective before it loses its potency, Esteban?" Amarilis asked, her voice revealing a calculated curiosity.

Esteban, unsuspecting, answered confidently:

"Well, I think ricin does not degrade as a molecule over time definitively. I believe its effectiveness lasts for many years," he paused and then added, "The military stores it for use in retaliation with chemical material."

Amarilis took in this new information, realizing the long-lasting potential of ricin. She knew she was handling an extremely dangerous substance and that, with the knowledge Esteban provided, her ability to use it was even greater. Esteban, absorbed in his scientific passion, continued explaining details about the stability of ricin and its potential use, unaware of the implications his words could have in Amarilis's mind.

The stability of ricin, combined with its lethality and the possibility of administering it along with epinephrine, offered a disturbing prospect. Amarilis, as she listened to Esteban, reflected on the multiple facets of the toxin and its applications, both beneficial and dark. The information she obtained not only served her studies but also fed the darkest corners of her mind.

"It's fascinating how something so small can be so powerful and long-lasting," Amarilis commented, trying to keep her voice neutral.

"That's right," Esteban responded, smiling. "The science behind these molecules is incredible, and their potential, though dangerous, can also be used for good, like in the development of antidotes and treatments."

Amarilis nodded, her mind working feverishly. She knew that the combination of ricin and epinephrine, and her ability to store the toxin indefinitely, opened a range of possibilities both in her work and her dark impulses. The line between her professional devotion and her distorted view of mercy blurred more and more, while Esteban remained unaware, lost in his world of research and scientific discoveries.

Little by little, undermining Esteban's laboratory, Amarilis began acquiring small liquid portions of ricin, which she then mixed in equal parts with epinephrine taken from the crash cart ampoules. With meticulous caution, she stored these mixtures for her personal use. She planned to use one milliliter in a tuberculin syringe to inject the IV fluids of newborns who were tired of living an agony due to their lethal genetic and congenital conditions.

Each time Esteban was distracted in the laboratory, Amarilis seized the opportunity to extract tiny amounts of ricin, ensuring that its absence went unnoticed. The combination with epinephrine, discreetly taken during her shifts in the NICU, was prepared with chilling precision. Amarilis knew this mixture was lethally effective, causing a rapid collapse without leaving obvious signs of poisoning.

The tuberculin syringes, small and precise, became her tools to carry out her macabre plan. In the silence of her apartment, Amarilis organized her inventory, labeling each syringe and storing them in a safe place. Her mind, divided between distorted compassion and cold calculation, drove her to act in what she considered a way to alleviate suffering.

Every time a baby with a lethal condition was admitted to the NICU, Amarilis watched with a mix of empathy and resolution. She saw the pain in the parents' eyes, the struggle in the tiny bodies of the newborns, and convinced herself that she was doing the right thing. In her mind, she was a liberator, a figure of mercy in a world of incessant suffering.

During her night shifts, when vigilance was lower and the hospital fell into an eerie silence, Amarilis acted. With cold, calculated precision, she injected the lethal mixture into the IV fluids of babies who, according to her, were destined for a life of pain and despair. She ensured the dose was enough to cause death without leaving obvious signs of poisoning, relying on her knowledge and the information she had extracted from Esteban.

The NICU, once a place of hope and the fight for life, had become the stage for Amarilis's dark mission. The monitors continued their rhythmic beeping, the mechanical respirators softly whispered, but beneath this facade of normalcy, the shadow of Amarilis moved stealthily.

Amarilis knew she had to be extremely careful. Any mistake could expose her and lead to unimaginable consequences. But her conviction was unshakeable, and every life she took was, to her, an act of mercy, a release from a cruel fate.

Meanwhile, Esteban remained unaware of Amarilis's actions. In the laboratory, he continued his research, oblivious to the fact that his discoveries were being used in such a sinister way. The trust and love he felt for Amarilis blinded him to the darkness that loomed over their relationship.

Time moved on, and the presence of Leticia Moran in the hospital increased the pressure. The investigator remained vigilant, determined to unravel the mystery behind the unexplained deaths. Amarilis, aware of the threat Leticia represented, became increasingly cautious, but her impulse to act remained strong.

The duality of her life, torn between the love she felt for Esteban and the dark deeds she committed, slowly consumed her. She knew the day of reckoning was approaching, and each step she took brought her closer to the precipice. But in her mind, each action was justified by a twisted sense of mercy, and she was willing to continue, no matter the cost.

VI

After six months of tense calm, another inexplicable death occurred in the NICU, this time right under the watchful eye of the eminent Leticia Moran. The victim was a premature baby of twenty-six weeks' gestation. Born with respiratory distress due to a congenital diaphragmatic hernia, which was successfully repaired on his second day of life, he weighed 1700 grams and was starting to overcome his pulmonary hypoplasia. He had a promising future if no complications arose, but unfortunately, complications did arise.

The baby developed an infection at the surgical site, resulting in sepsis and an open wound that oozed. The infection worsened when a piece of intestine got trapped in the closure of the abdominal wall, creating a high enterocutaneous fistula with a lot of intestinal content. Unable to ingest food due to the fistula, he was given total parenteral nutrition through a central vein.

One morning, the baby was found without vital signs during the shift change in front of everyone working in the NICU. Amarilis was not on duty at the time but had been there the previous day, administering her "merciful medications" to the little patient slowly enough to trigger the effect twelve hours or more later. She had a perfect alibi.

The news of the baby's death spread quickly, causing shock and sadness among the staff. Leticia Moran, who had been closely monitoring the situation, was immediately informed and began reviewing records and security footage. Every detail had to be analyzed precisely to find any clue about what had happened.

"This can't be a coincidence," Leticia murmured to herself as she examined the notes in the file. The sequence of events didn't make sense; the baby had shown signs of improvement, and the intravenous feeding should have stabilized his condition.

Amarilis, meanwhile, maintained her facade of professionalism and compassion. She knew Leticia was close to the truth but also trusted the meticulousness of her actions. She had administered the lethal mixture with chilling precision, ensuring the effects manifested after her shift ended.

The NICU team was in shock. The baby had been a symbol of hope, fighting against the odds since birth. Sadness and frustration mixed with a growing sense of helplessness. Leticia called an urgent meeting with the entire staff to discuss the events and emphasize the importance of remaining vigilant.

"This is a critical moment," Leticia said, her voice firm but full of empathy. "We need to be more vigilant than ever. The death of this baby cannot go unexplained. We will review every procedure, every detail, and we will not rest until we find the truth."

The tension in the NICU increased. The staff, aware of the gravity of the situation, redoubled their efforts to follow protocols to the letter. Leticia continued her tireless investigation, reviewing security footage and medication records. She knew the answer was somewhere between those pages and videos.

Amarilis, although confident in her alibi, felt the weight of constant surveillance. Every move was watched, every action documented. But her conviction remained firm; for her, freeing the babies from suffering was an act of mercy, even though the reality of her actions was much more sinister.

The NICU, a place of hope and the fight for life, was now shrouded in an atmosphere of distrust and fear. Leticia Moran, with her unyielding determination, continued her search for the truth, while Amarilis, hidden behind her mask of professionalism, awaited the next moment to act. The denouement was approaching, and the truth, no matter how dark, was about to come to light.

Leticia Moran meticulously reviewed her investigation dossier, searching for any clues she might have missed. Despite her thorough review of medical records, security footage, and staff interviews, she still lacked key pieces to solve the puzzle. There was no direct physical evidence indicating that someone was injecting the newborns with lethal substances. The syringes, medication residues, and visible traces on the babies' bodies were nonexistent, leaving a significant void in her investigation.

Despite exhaustive interviews, no staff member had noticed anything suspicious enough to point to a culprit. The lack of eyewitnesses who could link someone to the critical moments before the deaths left Leticia in frustrating uncertainty. She had found patterns in the timing of the deaths and the presence of certain staff members, but nothing that could directly implicate anyone. Without a clear suspect, these clues were fragmentary and inconclusive.

As she reflected on what she might have overlooked in her search, Leticia knew there was always a justification behind the actions, no matter how twisted they were. Her agile mind reviewed the possible reasons someone might have for harming the babies. She realized she had not thoroughly investigated who had frequent and unrestricted access to the crash cart medications. Although the cameras covered common areas, dark corners and furtive actions could have gone unnoticed.

She needed to conduct a deeper analysis of shifts and presences, looking for specific correlations between the presence of certain employees and critical moments. It could be that someone was manipulating the shift system to avoid suspicion. Additionally, the documentation of medication use might contain errors or subtle manipulations. Reviewing every record of medication entry and exit in more detail could reveal important inconsistencies.

Leticia focused on the possibility that someone was injecting the babies. Potential clues she might have overlooked included searching for micro-hematomas or tiny marks at injection sites, which could have been ignored or deemed insignificant during the initial autopsies. She also needed to conduct a more thorough analysis of the quantities of medications used and any discrepancies in the inventories that could be crucial. Although the babies had lethal conditions, the sudden onset of sepsis or complications could indicate the introduction of an external substance.

As these uncertainties flashed through Leticia's mind, she knew she also had to delve deeper into the possible justifications behind these acts. There could be someone who, in a twisted act of compassion, believed they were alleviating the babies' suffering. This motivation, though perverse, would have an internal logic for the perpetrator. A staff member with a traumatic past or who had experienced similar losses might be driven by a distorted view of compassion. Additionally, the high-pressure and constant stress environment in the NICU could push someone to the limit, leading them to justify extreme acts as a form of control or release.

These uncertainties flashed through Leticia's mind, aware that she was facing a difficult case to solve. She did not have a clear suspect, let alone a specific method, but her determination to uncover the truth did not waver. She knew she had to redouble her efforts, follow every lead no matter how small, and not rest until she found the culprit. The lives of the newborns depended on it, and justice, elusive as it seemed, was within reach if she kept investigating with the same tenacity and precision that had always characterized her.

In subsequent interviews with each staff member, Leticia began weaving a detailed investigation based on each individual's past, focusing on possible distortions of the human mind caused by childhood traumas. The questions were crafted by a psychologist friend, also a lesbian, with whom she had had a romantic relationship before her current judge partner. Leticia knew that something in the psyche of the person committing the crimes could provide the answer to why.

During these interviews, Leticia focused on understanding the personal histories and possible traumas of the employees better. She looked for signs of behavior patterns that could lead to a twisted act of "mercy." The psychologist friend, with her experience in childhood traumas, had helped formulate questions that could reveal hidden aspects of the interviewees' personalities.

However, Leticia still needed to determine the exact method the killer was using. She began investigating whether any staff member had any relationship with strange or unusual medications, especially those used in pharmaceuticals or chemical laboratories. She knew certain toxins could be invisible to the naked eye but lethal if administered properly.

An idea occurred to her: could arsenic be involved? Arsenic is known to be colorless, odorless, and clear. In its liquid form, it can be extremely difficult to detect and leaves no obvious traces except that it accumulates in hair strands. This characteristic made it an ideal poisoning agent for someone who wanted to go unnoticed.

Determined to explore this lead, Leticia sent a message to the forensic institute, requesting an analysis of the hair of the deceased newborns for the presence of arsenic. While waiting for the results, she continued her interviews, paying special attention to any indications that might link a staff member to the manipulation of chemicals or toxins.

The interviews were revealing. Some staff members had difficult family backgrounds, while others had gone through traumatic situations that had left deep scars on their psyches. Leticia, with the help of the psychological questions, began identifying behavior patterns and possible motivations that could be hidden behind a facade of professionalism and compassion.

As her investigation progressed, Leticia felt she was getting closer to the truth. The puzzle pieces were starting to fit together, although there were still many unanswered questions. The wait for the hair analysis results was nerve-wracking, but Leticia knew this test could be crucial in unmasking the culprit.

Amarilis, meanwhile, continued to perform her role with the same meticulous precision. Every time Leticia interviewed her, she maintained her impeccable professional facade, responding calmly and coherently. However, inside, she was increasingly aware that the net was closing in. The constant presence of Leticia and her thorough investigation were a growing threat.

The days passed, and the tension in the NICU increased. The staff, aware of the seriousness of the situation, fully cooperated with Leticia, although the shadow of distrust hung over everyone. Leticia continued to follow every lead, knowing that the denouement was near.

Finally, the results from the forensic institute arrived. To Leticia's surprise, the analysis of the newborns' hair did not reveal traces of arsenic. The results were negative, leaving Leticia without the lead she had hoped would be crucial. The disappointment was palpable, but she did not let it discourage her. She knew there had to be another method, another substance she was overlooking.

Determined to find the truth, Leticia went back to reviewing the files and medication records, looking for any indication of substances that could have been used inappropriately. She knew the killer must be using something less detectable, perhaps a combination of common medications that wouldn't raise immediate suspicion.

With renewed determination, Leticia decided to focus on the medications available in the NICU and their possible interactions. She meticulously reviewed the administered doses and the timing of the deaths, searching for patterns that might have been overlooked before.

The investigation now centered on those staff members with constant access to the medications, especially those with advanced knowledge in chemistry or pharmacology. The interviews began to delve into their skills and experiences, trying to find any detail that could provide a clue about the method used.

Meanwhile, Amarilis maintained her routine, aware that the net was tightening but also confident in her ability to conceal her actions. She knew arsenic wasn't her method, but that didn't mean she was safe. Leticia's constant presence kept her on guard, carefully adjusting each step to avoid raising suspicion.

The NICU remained a place of hope and struggle, but also of tension and distrust. Leticia Moran, with her relentless pursuit of the truth, would not rest until she unmasked the culprit. She knew the lives of the newborns depended on her ability to see what others could not, and she was determined to uncover the method and the mind behind these crimes.

VII

The staff interviews had not been a failure as Leticia initially thought. She had obtained valuable information from three nurses who had contact with places or chemical laboratories, and Amarilis was one of them.

The relationship between Esteban and Amarilis continued, though it had become a bit monotonous. Esteban, a lab rat, still had several months to finish a doctorate that seemed longer than the hope of a poor man. His dedication to research was admirable but also meant long hours of work and few opportunities to break the routine.

Every now and then, Amarilis stayed at Esteban's apartment, where they enjoyed each other's company. These moments were a respite from the constant stress of their studies and jobs. Other times, Amarilis retreated to the women's residence where she lived alone, although surrounded by other girls. The residence was a safe and quiet place, perfect for concentrating on her work and occasionally indulging in her dark thoughts.

At just twenty-three years old, Amarilis led a life divided between her job in the NICU, her relationship with Esteban, and her disturbing impulses. Her youth and apparent innocence allowed her to go unnoticed by most, but Leticia was beginning to see through the facade.

During one of the interviews, Leticia noticed something in the way Amarilis answered the questions. There was a calculated coldness, a precision in her responses that did not correspond to the gravity of the situation. This, along with the information that Amarilis had access to chemical laboratories, placed her at the center of Leticia's suspicions.

Meanwhile, Esteban was tirelessly working on his thesis. The research on ricin and its antidote consumed most of his time. Amarilis, taking advantage of her proximity to Esteban and her knowledge of the lab, continued to accumulate small amounts of ricin. She mixed the toxin with epinephrine, creating a lethal combination that she carefully stored for use.

Visits to Esteban's apartment were a mix of normalcy and tension. Although they enjoyed their time together, Amarilis always had a hidden agenda. Each time she was in the lab, she observed and learned, looking for any information that might be useful for her dark purposes. Esteban, completely unaware of her intentions, saw her as a companion and confidante.

In the women's residence, her roommates saw her as a reserved but kind young woman, dedicated to her work and in a stable relationship. However, Amarilis's mind was constantly divided between her public life and her hidden actions.

Leticia, for her part, continued her investigation with renewed determination. She knew she was close to discovering the truth. Each interview, each piece of information brought her closer to unmasking the culprit. Amarilis's connection to chemical laboratories and her precise, calculating behavior were clues that could not be ignored.

The atmosphere in the NICU remained tense. The staff, aware of the constant surveillance, followed their routines with heightened caution. The shadow of the unexplained deaths still hung over them, and Leticia's presence was a constant reminder that justice was on its way.

Amarilis, though aware that the noose was tightening, continued with her double life. Her youth and ability to manipulate those around her made her dangerous, and she knew she had to be extremely careful. Every action was calculated, every word measured. She knew that any mistake could be her end.

The truth was getting closer to coming to light, and Leticia would not rest until she unraveled the mystery. The lives of the newborns in the NICU depended on it, and justice, though elusive, was within reach if she continued to probe with the same tenacity and precision that had always characterized her.

Agent and doctor Leticia Moran decided to visit the facilities of the chemical laboratories where the three nurses in question had a connection. She knew that delving into the work environment of these women could reveal crucial clues about the chemicals being handled. Among the laboratories she visited, one of the most intriguing was Esteban's experimental lab, funded by the army to develop an antidote against an extremely potent biological and terrorist drug called ricin.

In each laboratory, Leticia meticulously observed the procedures and met with those in charge to understand the chemicals being handled. She realized that, besides ricin, there were other chemicals that could be potentially lethal if used improperly. Utilizing the artificial intelligence at her disposal, Leticia conducted quick and precise searches on the immediate reactions of all the chemicals that appeared in the laboratories of the three nurses.

The AI provided her with detailed information on the properties of each substance, its toxicity, and the possible combinations that could result in fatal outcomes. This analysis allowed her to identify patterns and connections that were not immediately evident.

At Esteban's lab, Leticia learned more about ricin and its devastating effects. She understood the details of Esteban's work and his team's efforts to develop an effective antidote. Leticia realized that ricin, combined with other chemicals like epinephrine, could be a nearly undetectable lethal weapon. This information reinforced her suspicion that Amarilis, with access to this lab and a deep knowledge of ricin, might be involved in the unexplained deaths in the NICU.

Leticia also discovered that the other two nurses worked in laboratories handling toxic and potent substances. Although there was no direct evidence implicating them, their constant access to these chemicals increased the likelihood of their involvement in something suspicious.

With each visit and conversation, Leticia got closer to understanding the full picture. The AI allowed her to correlate data and find patterns of behavior and substance use that would be impossible to detect manually. These findings were crucial for building a solid case against whoever was behind the deaths.

Meanwhile, Amarilis continued to play her part impeccably, though with increasing caution. She knew that Esteban's work in the lab was a constant source of information and resources for her, but also a dangerous connection that Leticia was beginning to unravel.

The visits to the labs and the use of advanced technology strengthened Leticia's conviction that she was on the right track. The interviews, behavior patterns, and access to lethal substances formed an increasingly clear picture in her mind. She knew she had to press on, pursuing every lead and not resting until she found the culprit.

The NICU continued to operate under an atmosphere of distrust and tension, but Leticia's presence was a beacon of hope for those seeking justice for the tiny patients. Amarilis, though cornered, maintained her facade, aware that any error could be her downfall.

The climax was approaching, and Leticia, with her combination of medical and investigative skills, was determined to uncover the truth. Every step she took brought her closer to unraveling the mystery and protecting the most vulnerable. The truth was within reach, and Leticia would not rest until justice prevailed.

In Leticia's analytical mind, the figure of Amarilis as the author of the fatal events in the NICU became increasingly palpable. Amarilis's past was marked by abuse and trauma inflicted by her stepfather, whose actions left her with deep emotional scars and a distorted perception of compassion. This unresolved childhood pain led her to develop a twisted sense of mercy, believing she was relieving the suffering of newborns condemned to lives of agony. There lay the suspect.

The likely method could have been the use of ricin, with or without another potent cardiovascular drug. Leticia knew that ricin was extremely lethal and, combined with something like epinephrine, would become a nearly undetectable lethal mixture in a standard autopsy. The idea that someone could use such specialized knowledge for such a sinister purpose filled her with a mix of horror and determination.

With this new hypothesis in mind, Leticia focused on gathering concrete evidence. She knew she needed more than suppositions to unmask Amarilis. She began to review the security recordings again, focusing on moments when Amarilis was alone in the NICU or near the crash cart where medications were stored. Additionally, she ordered a detailed review of access records to Esteban's lab and the controlled substances that could have been manipulated.

Every little detail could be crucial. Leticia knew that using ricin required careful preparation and that someone with constant access to Esteban's lab would have the perfect opportunity to obtain and prepare the toxin. As she reviewed the recordings, she looked for any hint of suspicious behavior, any movement that could betray the preparation or administration of the lethal substance.

Meanwhile, Amarilis continued her routine with the same meticulous precision. She showed no outward signs of nervousness, but inside she knew the noose was tightening. The constant presence of Leticia and the increased surveillance in the NICU made it increasingly difficult to carry out her plans. However, her conviction that she was doing the right thing, freeing babies from a life of suffering, drove her to continue.

During one of her visits to the lab, Leticia found a small but significant clue: a discrepancy in the records of controlled substances. Although minimal, this difference in the inventories indicated that something might have been diverted. Determined to follow this new lead, Leticia began correlating the dates of the discrepancies with Amarilis's shifts, looking for a pattern that could confirm her suspicions.

Time was running out, and Leticia knew it. Every day that passed without a resolution increased the risk for the tiny patients in the NICU. With a mix of determination and growing certainty, she prepared for the next step: a direct confrontation with Amarilis. She knew she needed to present her suspicions with enough evidence to pressure a confession or at least provoke a reaction that confirmed her theories.

The atmosphere in the NICU was tense. The staff, aware of the ongoing investigation, performed their tasks with extreme caution. Everyone knew that something dark had happened and that Leticia was close to uncovering the truth. Amarilis, though maintaining her facade of professionalism, felt the pressure intensify with each passing day.

Armed with her determination and the evidence she had gathered; Leticia knew she needed to catch Amarilis in the act. Everything happened so quickly in the NICU that it was essential to design a precise capture plan before another newborn lost their life. It was crucial to closely monitor the sickest patients, those who might be considered by Amarilis as candidates for her twisted mercy. Leticia and her team had to be alert to any baby in critical condition, watching if Amarilis attempted to act with her deadly "mercy serum."

With a clear focus, Leticia reinforced surveillance measures in the NICU. Additional cameras and motion sensors were installed around the incubators and medication carts. Constant monitoring shifts were also implemented, ensuring that there were always vigilant eyes on the most vulnerable patients. Any change in the babies' vital signs or suspicious movements by staff members would be reported immediately.

Amarilis, though aware of the increased security, could not resist her impulses. She knew she had to be extremely careful, but her conviction that she was freeing the babies from suffering drove her to continue. However, as the days passed, the pressure from the constant surveillance began to affect her.

Meanwhile, Leticia remained steadfast in her strategy. She knew she needed irrefutable evidence to unmask Amarilis. Every night, she meticulously reviewed the recordings, looking for patterns and any hint of tampering. Her experience and sharpness helped her detect even the most subtle movements that could betray Amarilis.

One night, Leticia noticed something that caught her attention. Amarilis had spent more time than usual near one of the medication carts and then approached the incubator of a critically ill baby. The sequence of movements was almost imperceptible, but enough to raise suspicions in Leticia's mind.

VIII

Apprehending a cunning and twisted mind is not easy. History is replete with judicial mistakes involving individuals who are innocent despite appearing guilty. In this situation, where healthcare professionals hold lives in their hands, a more coordinated plan was warranted to catch the real culprit.

Instead of acting immediately, Leticia decided to wait. She knew she had to be patient and let Amarilis incriminate herself with conclusive evidence. With her team, she reinforced surveillance around the incubator of any critically ill baby, ensuring that every move by Amarilis was monitored in real time.

During the following weeks, tension in the NICU was palpable. The staff, aware of the situation, performed their duties with extreme caution. Leticia and her team maintained constant vigilance, waiting for the moment when Amarilis would make a mistake. Each passing day increased the pressure, both for Leticia and for Amarilis.

Amarilis, although aware of the increased security, could not resist her impulses. She knew she had to be extremely careful, but her conviction that she was releasing babies from suffering drove her forward. Despite the intensified surveillance, her determination did not waver.

Meanwhile, Leticia focused her attention on the sickest newborns, those whom Amarilis might consider as "candidates" for her twisted form of mercy. Using artificial intelligence and collected data, Leticia identified patients with the most critical conditions and established a continuous monitoring system for them. She made sure to personally review camera recordings and medication records every day, looking for any signs of manipulation.

There was one particular baby whom everyone had grown fond of due to the extensive time spent in the unit. Born at twenty-four weeks and weighing 800 grams, he had a closed abdominal wall defect. In utero, he had lost a large portion of his small intestine. He relied on parenteral nutrition through a central vein because if he ingested food, he developed diarrhea. A gastrostomy tube had been placed due to a neurological deficit that had caused his brain's gray matter to be replaced by white matter.

Despite his numerous complications, this baby was beautiful, with a pointed nose and a social smile that warmed hearts in the NICU. He held nurses' hands and laughed, creating a special bond with the staff. When he reached a weight of over 2500 grams, he was taken to the operating room for a small intestine lengthening procedure. From the original twenty-three centimeters, they managed to extend it to forty-six.

The baby's parents were kind and grateful to all the nurses. Despite the bleak prognosis and the short gut problem, they remained hopeful. They knew that a temporary solution would be an intestine transplant, but they did not have the 2.3 million pesos needed for the operation. Furthermore, transplanted babies rarely survived more than five years. In this dilemma, the family found themselves trapped between hope and despair, clinging to the small light that their son represented in a sea of uncertainty.

Amarilis felt a special connection with this baby. His vulnerability and his parents' desperate situation resonated deeply in her heart. She saw in him a reflection of her own suffering and pain. Every time she attended to him, she couldn't help but feel a mix of compassion and sadness, knowing that his future was uncertain and likely painful. The shadow of her past clouded her perception, distorting her sense of mercy and leading her to question whether keeping these little beings alive was truly an act of kindness.

Leticia Moran's constant presence had led to a reduction in cases of mercy euthanasia in the NICU. However, Amarilis knew that the net was tightening. Surveillance was becoming increasingly intense, and the atmosphere was charged with tension with each passing day. She knew she had to be more careful than ever, but her conviction that she was alleviating suffering remained her guide.

She prayed to her karma to protect the lives of the suffering innocents. Amarilis considered herself compassionate and merciful to the most helpless, convinced that putting them on God's right hand would reduce their earthly condemnation. She firmly believed that she would alleviate the parents' daily suffering for the developmental errors they were not to blame for. All this tangled web of thoughts filled Amarilis's mind, who, in removing newborns from the earth, believed she was doing good for both the babies and their families.

Her distorted mind saw these acts as a compassionate service, a way to release the little ones from a life of pain and their parents from constant agony. Amarilis felt justified, convinced that her version of mercy was the right one. This exemplary nurse, admired for her dedication and care, concealed a deranged mental problem that drove her to dispense lethal mercy.

In the case of the baby with the abdominal wall defect and short gut, Amarilis felt particularly drawn. The parents' desperation, their daily struggle, and the baby's innocent gaze resonated in her heart. Amarilis, with her twisted perception of compassion, saw in this little one another victim of suffering she needed to alleviate. Her determination grew with every smile from the baby, with every gesture of affection she received from the staff.

Meanwhile, Leticia remained vigilant, analyzing every move by Amarilis and other staff members. She knew she had to be patient and gather conclusive evidence. The NICU had become a silent battlefield, where life and death hung by a thread, and where justice had to prevail.

Amarilis, despite the growing surveillance, continued with her mission. Every day, she assessed the sickest babies, calculating their movements with precision. She knew any mistake could expose her, but her conviction was unshakable. For her, freeing these babies from suffering was an act of love, a mercy only she could provide.

The atmosphere in the NICU was charged with tension. The staff, though professional, couldn't help but feel the constant pressure. Each of them was aware that something dark lurked among them, and Leticia's presence was a constant reminder that the truth would come to light.

Finally, one night, as Amarilis attended to the baby with the short gut, she felt a particular urgency. She watched as the little one struggled with his condition, as his parents clung to a fading hope. In her mind, the decision formed clear and definitive: she had to act.

She went to the crash cart and quietly took out a vial of epinephrine. Then she went to her belongings, where she extracted a small test tube containing the ricin that Esteban produced in his lab and that she had been stealing. She mixed both substances in equal parts and prepared the lethal mixture, putting half a milliliter of each into a tuberculin syringe.

She thought twice. It was four in the morning on a Tuesday, November 17th. It was just her and her fellow guard, both tired, but Amarilis always showed more spirit. With cold determination, she approached the baby's incubator with short intestine, her heart pounding with a mixture of nervousness and disturbed certainty.

With precise and calculated movements, Amarilis prepared to administer her lethal "mercy serum." Unbeknownst to her, Leticia and her team were watching every move in real-time using new video cameras installed in the unit. She approached the baby's incubator, her heart pounding with a mixture of determination and a disturbed sense of justice.

At the precise moment Amarilis was about to inject the lethal mixture into the baby's serum, Leticia gave the signal. The security team members burst into the room, arresting Amarilis in the act. Surprise and terror reflected on her face as she was caught in her attempt to commit another act of merciful euthanasia.

Immediately, Leticia and the attending staff removed the serum contaminated with poisons, ensuring it was swiftly sent to toxicology for detailed analysis. Leticia gave specific instructions to the toxicology lab to conduct tests for alpha agonists like epinephrine and ricin, the potent inhibitor of ribosomes in all body cells. She knew identifying these substances would be crucial to building a strong case against Amarilis.

Meanwhile, Amarilis was read her Miranda rights and escorted, handcuffed, straight to the police station, where they awaited to interrogate her as the prime suspect in the deaths that occurred in the unit. The cold expression on her face contrasted with the shock her arrest caused among the NICU staff.

The police station was prepared to receive Amarilis. Leticia, with a mixture of professionalism and determination, oversaw every step of the procedure. She knew she had to ensure everything was done according to the law to avoid any possible error that could jeopardize the justice the babies and their families deserved.

Amarilis, on the other hand, maintained an unsettling facade of calm as she was escorted. In her mind, the distorted justification of her actions remained firm, but now she faced the reality of her crimes under the cold, relentless light of justice.

In the interrogation room, Leticia observed from the other side of the one-way mirror. The atmosphere was tense, charged with an almost palpable anticipation. Amarilis, sitting with handcuffed hands in front of her, knew the moment to face her actions had come. The questions would be tough, the evidence damning, and the truth, however dark, would finally come to light.

IX

Once at the police station, Amarilis was entitled to a phone call to notify a lawyer or a family member. With her mother already dead due to her stepfather's abuse, she only had Esteban, her lab rat, who had taught her the chemistry of crime. Desperate and with a foggy mind, she made a call to the poor man. Esteban, more frightened than calm, immediately rushed to the police station where Amarilis was detained.

Amarilis's voice on the phone was cold and controlled, but Esteban, who knew her well, sensed the underlying panic. Upon arriving at the station, his hands trembled, and sweat beaded on his forehead. He had never faced anything so serious, and despite his intelligence, he felt completely lost.

When Esteban arrived, he was greeted by an officer who guided him to a waiting room. There, he observed through the glass Amarilis, sitting with her hands handcuffed and her gaze fixed on the floor. His heart sank at the sight, and for a moment, he couldn't reconcile the image of the woman he loved with the suspect of multiple deaths.

Leticia, aware of Esteban's arrival, prepared to interrogate Amarilis with the same precision and coldness with which she had conducted the entire investigation. She knew Esteban's presence might provoke useful reactions for the case. She was determined to obtain a full confession and clarify all the details of Amarilis's actions.

While Esteban waited, his mind filled with questions. How had it come to this? What role had he truly played in Amarilis's crimes? Guilt began to consume him. Although he hadn't committed the murders, his knowledge and teachings had provided the tools she needed.

Finally, he was allowed to see Amarilis. The atmosphere in the interrogation room was tense, charged with suppressed emotions. Esteban sat across from Amarilis, and for a moment, they both looked at each other in silence, words stuck in their throats.

"Esteban," began Amarilis, her voice barely a whisper.

"I need you to understand... I did it to alleviate their suffering."

Esteban, with eyes filled with confusion and pain, could only nod. There were no words that could justify what she had done, and yet, in her twisted logic, she firmly believed it.

Leticia entered the room, her imposing presence breaking the silence. With a firm voice, she began detailing the evidence they had against Amarilis, each word another nail in the coffin of the justification she had built.

Unable to bear it any longer, Esteban stood up and left the room, leaving her alone with the reality of her crimes. Outside, leaning against the wall, he tried to compose himself. The woman he loved was a murderer, and he, in a way, had been her unwitting accomplice.

The night closed in on the police station as Leticia continued her interrogation. Amarilis, trapped between her twisted logic and the harsh reality, began to understand the magnitude of her actions. Justice was near, and the truth, painful as it was, would finally come to light.

Several of the newborns' bodies were exhumed, victims of the mercy cocktail. Leticia knew that to confirm her suspicions about Amarilis's method, she needed conclusive scientific evidence. She ordered specific tests on the baby's blood samples, opting for a combination of ELISA and mass spectrometry. These advanced techniques would detect and quantify the presence of ricin with unparalleled precision.

The toxicology laboratory received Leticia's detailed instructions. The technicians began the ELISA assay, using specific antibodies to identify any trace of the toxin. Mass spectrometry, with its ability to identify and quantify small amounts of substances, would complement the results, providing irrefutable confirmation.

The results soon arrived. The laboratory screen showed unmistakable peaks corresponding to ricin, and the ELISA analysis corroborated the presence of the toxin at lethal levels. With this evidence, Leticia had the scientific proof she needed to strengthen her case against Amarilis.

Everyone had abandoned the murderer. The woman who had been mistreated as a child and who had decided to impart mercy among the little ones now was at the mercy of justice. She had no friendly lawyer. The state provided her legal representation. Attorney Arnaldo Rivera would handle her case, although she was in a daze, incredulous of what she already knew would happen.

Arnaldo Rivera, a court-appointed lawyer with years of experience in complex cases, sat across from Amarilis in the police station's visiting room. He looked at her carefully, trying to understand the woman behind the crimes. Amarilis, with vacant eyes and a mind trapped in her own world, barely reacted to his presence.

"Mrs. Cintron, I'm Attorney Rivera. I'm here to represent you," he said firmly but kindly, trying to connect with her. Amarilis slowly looked up, her eyes showing a glimmer of recognition and, for a brief moment, vulnerability.

"It doesn't matter what I do, I'm already condemned," murmured Amarilis, her voice broken but resigned.

"I did what I believed was right, but now everyone sees me as a monster."

Arnaldo took a deep breath. He knew this case would not be easy, neither legally nor emotionally. He had read the reports, the evidence, and knew the accusations against Amarilis. His task was to search for any hint of humanity in her, something he could use to build a defense.

"My job is to make sure you have a fair trial," Arnaldo replied calmly. "I need you to tell me everything that happened, without omitting any details. Every piece of information can be crucial."

Amarilis nodded slowly, her thoughts swirling between the past and the present. She began to speak, her voice initially hesitant but gaining strength as she remembered the events that had led her here. She described her childhood full of abuse, the pain she had endured, and how that had shaped her view of compassion and mercy.

As he listened, Arnaldo took detailed notes. He knew he had to find a balance between the harsh reality of the crimes and Amarilis's traumatic background. Although the evidence against her was overwhelming, her human story could be a key piece in court, offering at least an understanding of the why behind her actions.

The judicial process would be long and arduous. Leticia, for her part, prepared to present the conclusive scientific evidence linking Amarilis to the deaths in the NICU. The results of the toxicology tests, confirming the presence of ricin and epinephrine in the babies' serums, would be the central axis of the accusation.

The day of the trial arrived quickly. The courtroom was filled with reporters, relatives of the victims, and hospital staff, all waiting to see how the case would unfold. Arnaldo and Amarilis entered, she with her gaze low and he with a professional determination on his face.

Leticia, sitting among the audience, watched attentively. She knew this trial would not only bring justice to the victims but also close a dark chapter in the hospital's history. The truth, with all its harshness, was about to be revealed.

Arnaldo rose to make his opening statement, aware of the difficult task ahead. He looked at the jury members, at the judges, and began to speak, carefully weaving the narrative of a broken woman, a victim of her own past, who had made terrible decisions in the name of a distorted perception of mercy.

"Ladies and gentlemen of the jury," he began, with a firm yet compassionate voice. "Today, we are not only here to judge the actions of Amarilis Cintron, but also to understand why behind them. She is not a monster, but a person trapped in a cycle of pain and desperation, seeking relief in the only way she knew."

The trial continued, each testimony and each piece of evidence painting a complex and somber picture. Amarilis, in her corner, faced the consequences of her actions, aware that her story and her life were now in the hands of justice.

As the trial progressed, I couldn't help but follow every detail, every testimony, and every piece of evidence presented. Attorney Arnaldo Rivera did his best to humanize Amarilis, showing her history of suffering and the twisted logic that had led her to her actions. The prosecution, on the other hand, presented the evidence with cold and meticulous precision, ensuring that the truth would come to light.

The toxicology test results confirmed the presence of ricin and epinephrine in the babies' serums. The security footage showed Amarilis manipulating the medications. Every piece of evidence was another blow, reaffirming the magnitude of her crimes.

Deep down, I couldn't help but feel a mix of compassion and sadness for Amarilis. I knew she was beyond any justification, but I couldn't help but remember the dedicated and kind nurse I had known. The woman who had believed in relieving suffering, albeit in a completely distorted and deadly way.

The courtroom was filled with whispers every time a new detail was mentioned. The parents of the victims, visibly affected, followed the trial with looks full of pain and anger. Their lives had been devastated by someone they trusted to care for their children. My heart ached for them, feeling their desperation and their search for justice.

Dr. Lucio Vicens, who had been called to testify, spoke with a voice broken by emotion. He described how he trusted Amarilis, how he had never suspected her intentions. His testimony, filled with remorse and sadness, resonated deeply with all of us.

As the trial continued, the image of Amarilis blurred between compassion and horror. She knew she must face the consequences of her actions, but she couldn't help feeling that somehow, we had all failed to see the signs, to help her before it was too late.

Justice would follow its course, but the hospital, the staff, and all of us who knew Amarilis would be forever marked by this tragedy. And I, amidst it all, would continue to seek answers, trying to understand how such a dedicated woman could fall into the darkness of lethal mercy.

The court determined that Amarilis was guilty of the premeditated murder of twelve newborns over a period of five years. It was a devastating blow to the parents, the institution, and the healthcare staff. The verdict was clear: she was to serve a life sentence without the possibility of parole in the women's penitentiary in the south of the country.

The news spread quickly, causing a wave of shock and sadness. The parents of the victims, present in the courtroom, broke down in tears upon hearing the verdict. Their tears reflected the profound and irreparable pain they carried in their hearts. For them, there was no solace in justice, only an acknowledgment of the tragedy that had robbed them of their children.

At the National Pediatric Hospital, the atmosphere turned somber. The healthcare staff, who had worked side by side with Amarilis, were in a state of shock. The trust and respect they had once held for her had turned into a mixture of disbelief and horror. The nurse who had been seen as a role model turned out to be a murderer.

Dr. Heriberto Lucio Vicens, my mentor, was particularly affected. Guilt and remorse tormented him, reminding him of every decision and praise he had given Amarilis. In the hospital corridors, his words resonated with palpable sadness: "I never would have imagined... Amarilis was one of the best. Always attentive, always concerned about the little ones."

Meanwhile, in the women's penitentiary, Amarilis faced a new reality. The gray walls and iron bars were a constant reminder of her crimes and the price she had to pay. Although she maintained a calm facade, her mind was a whirlwind of thoughts and emotions. Inside, she struggled with accepting her fate and the distorted logic that had led her to commit those atrocious acts.

Arnaldo Rivera, her defense attorney, withdrew from the case with a bitter feeling. He had done everything possible to humanize Amarilis, to present her story of suffering and justify, even partially, her actions. However, the magnitude of her crimes was undeniable, and justice had spoken.

For me, the news of Amarilis's verdict and sentence was a deep blow. During my training as a surgeon, I had witnessed her dedication and care for the patients. The image of the kind and committed nurse had faded, leaving only the reality of a woman broken by her own past and decisions.

The Neonatal Intensive Care Unit (NICU), once a place of hope and life, was now marked by the shadow of Amarilis's crimes. The staff moved forward, trying to find solace in their daily work, but the wound was deep and would take time to heal. Every incubator, every little patient, reminded them of the price of betrayed trust.

Dr. Lucio Vicens, in an attempt to find some peace, immersed himself in his work with renewed intensity. He knew he had to move forward for the sake of the other patients and their families. But every night, when the hospital lights went out, the ghosts of the lost children and Amarilis's betrayal visited him, reminding him of the fragility of life and the importance of constant vigilance.

The sentence of Amarilis was a brutal reminder that even the most sacred and secure places can be violated. Justice had prevailed, but the pain and impact of her actions would linger on all who had once trusted her. And I, amidst it all, continued to seek answers, trying to understand how someone so close could fall into darkness, leaving a legacy of sadness and desolation.

Ten years had passed since that lamentable true story, and my practice as a surgeon was thriving. However, one day I read a news that deeply shook me: a prisoner had committed suicide in the penitentiary. The details of the news spoke of a nurse named Amarilis Cintron, who in her anguish and depression had deprived herself of life.

The headline of the article was direct and cold, but the following words were laden with a sadness and desperation that made me remember everything we had lived through. Amarilis Cintron, the woman whose story had shaken the medical community and left an indelible scar on the National Pediatric Hospital, had made a final decision.

The news recounted how Amarilis, in the last years, had fallen into a deep depression. The psychologists of the penitentiary tried to help her, but her mind, trapped in a tangle of remorse and pain, seemed beyond salvation. In her final letters, addressed to no one in particular, she spoke of her days in the NICU, of the children she had cared for, and, tragically, of those she had taken from the world with her own hand.

I sat at my desk, the article still open on my computer screen. The images of those years flooded back into my mind: the faces of the grieving parents, the hospital staff trying to process the betrayal, and the endless nights when we tried to make sense of what had happened. Amarilis had been a colleague, a friend to some, and her fall into darkness had left a mark on all of us.

The article mentioned that Amarilis had been found in her cell, with a peaceful expression on her face that she hadn't shown in years. She had left a note, brief and simple, that said: "Forgive me. I couldn't bear it anymore." That line, so simple and heartbreaking, resonated in my mind over and over again.

I stood up and walked to the window of my office, looking out at the horizon. Life had continued, but the shadow of that tragedy was still present. I thought of Dr. Lucio Vicens, how he had tried to cope with guilt and pain. I thought of the parents who never got their children back, and the young patients who never had the chance to grow up.

Amarilis's death closed a dark and painful chapter, but it also opened the door to a deeper reflection on compassion, justice, and forgiveness. I realized that, despite everything, there was a lesson to be learned from this tragedy: the importance of vigilance, of caring not only for patients but also for ourselves and our colleagues.

I decided that night I would visit the hospital. I wanted to see the new patients, talk to the new generations of nurses and doctors, and remind them of the importance of empathy and care. I knew that, somehow, this tragedy had to serve a greater purpose, to prevent something similar from happening again.

In the hospital, life went on. Babies in the incubators, parents worried but hopeful, and staff working tirelessly to provide the best possible care. In those young and determined faces, I found a ray of hope.

As I left the hospital, under the starry night sky, I felt a mixture of sadness and resolve. The story of Amarilis Cintron was a warning and a reminder of the fragility of the human condition. Although her life had ended tragically, the legacy of her story should be a call to empathy, to vigilance, and above all, to true compassion.

* * *

X

About the Author

Born on April 14, 1954, in San Juan, Puerto Rico, Dr. Humberto Lugo Vicente, better known as Tito Lugo, is a distinguished figure in the field of pediatric surgery. His career has been distinguished by a fervent commitment to both medicine and the community he serves.

During his education at Colegio San José de Río Piedras, Dr. Lugo Vicente not only excelled in his studies but also led the local rock band "The Red Stones." He demonstrated exceptional skills in areas as varied as music and martial arts, where he achieved black belts in Shotokan and brown belts in Taekwondo. His determination to finance his karate education through newspaper sales and other jobs reflects his early commitment to his goals.

A graduate of the University of Puerto Rico Magna Cum Laude in Science, specializing in Chemistry and Biochemistry, Dr. Lugo Vicente was recognized with the Chemistry Medal and the Facundo Bueso Medal for his outstanding academic performance. He continued to shine in his medical studies at the same university, graduating as a member of Alpha Omega Alpha, the medical honor society.

Dr. Lugo Vicente has made a milestone in pediatric surgery throughout his career. He completed his specialization in General and Pediatric Surgery at the University of Puerto Rico. He then joined the faculty as Professor of Pediatric Surgery. His commitment to excellence in education led him to hold several leadership positions, including President of the Medical Faculty and Director of the Department of Surgery at the University Pediatric Hospital.

Dr. Lugo Vicente has been a tireless advocate for improving medical services in Puerto Rico, especially in his fight to equip the University Pediatric Hospital with modern operating rooms. This has benefited countless children and families.

Outside of his medical career, he enjoys an enriching family life with his wife Wanda Torres Otero and their four children: Karlos, Alex, Javier, and María del Carmen. His dedication to community well-being and his passion for medicine continue to be a source of inspiration for new generations.

Currently, Dr. Lugo Vicente practices in his private practice at Hospital San Jorge and the University Pediatric Hospital. There, he provides quality medical care while cultivating his interests in sports, writing, and oenology, always maintaining the balance and moderation that characterize his philosophy of life.

Other novels from the Author
https://www.amazon.com/author/titolugo.md

1- Aquamistic (Spanish and English)
2- El Gran Sueño / The Great Dream
3- Marca de Faraón / Mark of Pharaoh
4- La Isla del Retiro / The Island of Retirement
5- Espejismos en la Red / Digital Deceptions
6- Voces del Silencio / Voices of Silence
7- Travos... (Spanish and English)
8- Misericordia Letal / Lethal Mercy